Gaby and
The Best Middle School
Self-Defense Book Ever

Gaby and
The Best Middle School
Self-Defense Book Ever

by

Linda Elkin

ISBN: 1499767080
ISBN 13: 9781499767087
Library of Congress Control Number: 2014910287
CreateSpace Independent Publishing Platform
North Charleston, South Carolina

For Larry
For Jess and Ali
For all of the wonderful Gabys and Lilys
who have filled our lives

squeak, squeak, squeak

9/1 - Thursday

So my mom says that sometimes you have to be your own best friend.

I started seventh grade today, and the same annoying crew was there to greet me. The "populars" in their new school gear were in the hall waiting for their full crowd before making their grand entrance into the gym. I squeezed through all of the conversations, found a spot by the wall in the gym, and waited for my best friends to show. I hadn't seen them all summer. Lindsay had been away at sleep-away camp and then left for a family vacation. Taylor also had been away, visiting cousins for most of the summer. I went on a cross-country trip with my family and barely made it home without wanting to suffocate everyone in the car. Well, not everyone. My dog had been reasonably pleasant.

I thought that I would hang out with Taylor and Lindsay during the week before school started, but plans kept getting messed up. I called a few times, but only got their voicemail. When we texted back and forth, they were always busy with one thing or another.

Anyway, Tay and Lins walked in together, saw me, and then made a beeline for the other side of the gym. I just wanted to die. There I was, alone, with no one to talk to. Our names were all called, and homeroom locations were handed out. I rushed out of the gym to my new homeroom. Life wasn't much better there. None of my friends from sixth grade were in my homeroom, even if I was desperate and counted Lindsay and Taylor. We sat in alphabetical order, and I wound up next to Lily, one of the most unpopular girls in our grade.

After a long day, skipping lunch and hiding out in the library, I raced home and hid in my room. I'm really glad this is a short week.

I'm not really sure what this "own best friend" stuff is about. Maybe it means that sometimes you won't have anyone to count on but yourself, so you better figure out how to enjoy being alone. If that's what she means, then she could be right.

So—*maybe*, I'll try what my mom said and just be my own best friend for a little while.

9/6 - Tuesday of torment

Sat alone again at lunch on Friday and today. At least Labor Day was yesterday, and it's another short week. I'm beginning to wonder if I'll ever have a friend again. I don't know what is going on or why I'm alone all of the time, but this really stinks! Taylor and Lindsay haven't responded to any of my texts or phone calls. Whenever I see them, they're hanging out with the populars and pretending that they don't see me.

Ms. Lamb—yep, when she isn't too close, you can hear a lot of kids baa-ing—is a pretty good language arts teacher. She's having us create our own nonfiction book about anything we want. I have to figure this out.

In the meantime, Lily isn't so bad. She's in some classes with me, and we walk together. She dresses kind of strange, like my mom, and has this bag, I think designer, that she stuffs with candy. She gave me a Jolly Rancher and some M&Ms during math. I saw her at lunch, also sitting alone. I hoped that some of my old friends, any of them, would join me. No such luck. Next week I just might have to eat with Lily.

9/8 - Thursday and dragging

Alone at lunch again—until Lily plopped herself next to me and started chatting away about her summer and her trips to some fancy place, and her dog. (The dog's name is Wonder Woman—Wonder for short—really?) I just smiled and nodded which is what my dad says that he does a lot. But it was nice to have someone to talk to, even though she did most of the talking.

I'm still looking for a book idea for my language arts project. Ms. Lamb says we can work with another person if we want. I'm lying low because I think Lily has her eye on me. Whenever she brings up the project, I change the subject. We'll see.

9/9 - Friday, finally

Still no one around to hang out with but Lily. I'm starting to get used to the idea that she may be it this year. She had Tootsie Rolls with her today and snuck some to me during homeroom. I'm actually looking forward to having lunch with her.

We hang out outside and walk around after lunch before we have language arts. I still have no idea what to do for the semester project. Book ideas are due Monday.

It still bothers me that Tay and Lins could just stop wanting to be around me. I guess some signs were there before the summer. There had been a few times when I thought I had plans with them, but they just didn't show. There were always excuses like, "Oh! You meant yesterday? Oops! We thought you meant tomorrow" and, "Oh, but tomorrow won't work. We have stuff going on." I just thought nothing of it, or maybe I wanted to think nothing of it. I'm thinking a lot more of it now.

9/10 - Saturday, sigh

So last night Lily texted me. She said she had a great idea for the project and asked if I wanted to work on it with her. Since she ambushed me and I had no ideas, I sighed and texted, "Okay what?"

She called.

"Hey, Gaby, let's write a book that gives advice on all of the problems kids our age have," she said excitedly.

"Huh? How can *we* give advice when *we* have most of the problems kids our age have?" I said way less excitedly.

"Do you have any ideas for the project?" she asked.

"Not really."

"So let's do it."

I felt kind of nervous. Telling Lily that I'd do this meant that we would be working on this project together for the whole fall semester. That's a long time to spend with someone you're not really sure that you want to be friends with in the first place. I didn't have any other ideas, though, and I don't actually have any other friends at the moment, so I said, "Well, okay."

"Great," she said. "I'll e-mail Ms. Lamb tonight and see if she approves it."

"Wait…Can't we wait until tomorrow?"

There was a pause at the other end of the phone, and Lily said, "Are you waiting for someone better to come along?"

What could I do? I lied. "No. Oh fine! Go ahead." I hung up and went downstairs to see what my weird family was doing.

Meet the weird family. My mom jokes a lot and dances around the house doing Zumba. She is a work-part-time-with-my-dad mom, so she's around a lot more than most kids' moms. This can be good and bad. She's pretty available to take me places, but she's here more than I want, particularly when something is wrong. She asks too many questions that I don't feel like answering, especially this year.

My dad reads a lot. He reads everything, everywhere. We can't walk into a museum without expecting to be there for hours. Some of this summer's trip was absolutely excruciating because we had to wait forever for Dad to read everything, everywhere.

My older sister, Audrey, is brilliant. Everyone says so, and she does too. She's always studying and is already planning what college she wants to go to, and she's only in tenth grade. She stresses me out by just being around.

My dog, Scout, is my favorite. All she wants to do is cuddle, and that's all I want to do when I get home from school, so we're great together.

When I went downstairs, my mom immediately started asking me questions about my day, my friends, my homework, my lunch, and on and on. I grabbed my backpack and tried to go back upstairs.

"So did you figure out your language arts project?" Mom asked.

"I think so. I'm going to work with Lily, and we're going to write a self-help book for middle schoolers about their problems."

Audrey snorted and looked up from her double-extra-advanced math book.

"Really? You?"

"Audrey, enough," Mom said.

Audrey rolled her eyes and went back to her double-double extra.

"Well, that sounds very interesting, sweetie. Good luck," Mom said, trying to be encouraging. Dad smiled and nodded, as usual.

"Yeah, good luck with that," Audrey said, I think sarcastically, but it was hard to tell because everything she says sounds that way.

I got a text back from Lily and it said, "Great news! Ms. Lamb e-mailed. Says it's a go."

"Wonderful." I groaned. Everyone looked up, but I walked out of the room and went upstairs.

Enough about last night.

9/12 - Monday, sad

When I woke up for school today, I had this feeling of dread. I was committed to this project, with this person, for the whole semester. I really don't relish the idea of any of it and I'm stuck. But I really don't want to work alone. I'm tired of being alone so much.

Lily was incredibly cheerful at school. I just wanted the day to end so I could go home, snuggle with Scout, and hide.

In class I faced one of the most mortifying days of my life. Ms. Lamb read out all of the topics to the class, and when she got to our topic, the class went wild. They thought it was so funny that someone like Lily and someone like me could pretend to be "experts" on middle school problems. I wished that I had never met Lily. Ms. Lamb calmed the class down and talked a lot about camaraderie while I tried not to cry.

Lily looked and me and said, "We'll show them all!" I tried to look as certain as she did but felt my lunch bubbling in my stomach. Ms. Lamb had us break into our writing groups. It seemed like most of the class had teamed up.

Lily said, "Okay, the chapter outline is due next week, so let's get started."

"Great," I said. "First problem to solve. What do you do when everyone thinks that you're weird, and everything you do says that they're right?" Lily looked like she wanted to strangle me, but instead she snuck a Life Saver.

"Aren't you going to offer me one?" I asked.

"Only if you stop being so afraid and forget about everyone else!" she retorted.

Now I wanted to strangle *her*, but I was really in the mood for a Life Saver, and so I said, "Fine. So what should we do?"

Lily savored her candy. "Let's make a list of all the problems that there are."

"We'll never leave this room!" I said.

Lily glared at me. "Come on!"

So we started:

> Girls don't like me.
> I don't know how to make friends. I'm too shy.
> Boys don't like me.

"I hope that changes," Lily said.

"Yeah. Me too," I replied.

> My parents drive me crazy.
> My mom won't buy me cool clothes.

Lily didn't see cool clothes as much of a problem of hers.

> I have too much homework. School stresses me
> out.

I am getting bullied. What do I say to a mean person?
My friends stopped wanting to be with me.

That last one I contributed.

"Time's up," Ms. Lamb said. "Now, in addition to creating your topic list or outline, I want you to create a research plan. This will be due on Wednesday. This means that you have to go out into the field and get thoughts from at least three other classmates on whether your topics are of interest, and then have them suggest two additional topics of their own that they are interested in."

I looked at Ms. Lamb. Now she was the one I wanted to strangle. I could barely find one person to talk to. How was I going to find others? And it's not like Lily was Miss Popularity herself.

Lily looked at me and shrugged. "Hey, this will be soooo easy. Everyone has a favorite problem."

"And they're just dying to share their problems with us? Lily, really!"

"We'll see. Let's try right after school to ask some kids."

I knew what to expect. I followed Lily around after school as she tried to get kids to tell her their problems. She started with other seventh graders, and then sixth, and even the fifth graders. No one wanted to tell us anything. Even bribes from her "magic bag of treats" didn't work. We walked home from school really discouraged. Just as we were about to head our separate ways, I thought of something.

"Let's put a sign up tomorrow and appeal to the whole school. We'll ask kids to pick their worst problem and e-mail it anonymously to us. This way no one else has to know they helped us."

"What do they get in return?" Lily asked. Her exuberant polling mood had vanished.

"We can just thank them," I said.

"Now I think that you're nuts."

"Well, we need input from other kids, and I don't know any other way."

"We also have to get feedback about our topics," she said.

"Aaaagh, I don't know! Let's just do this."

We decided that we'd put up signs before school started tomorrow. They would read:

PLEASE HELP ON AN IMPORTANT PROJECT

Please e-mail your biggest problem to one of
the addresses below by tomorrow. You will be
anonymous (sort of).

I wasn't happy with the "sort of" part, but Lily felt that no one could really be anonymous if they were using their e-mail addresses, and then she gave me a big speech about truth in advertising. I had no idea what she meant; I just surrendered. I'm starting to learn that surrendering is less painful.

9/13 - tense Tuesday

Lily and I arrived at school really early to put up our signs. The rest of the day went by pretty quickly. I was relieved and at the same time disappointed to discover that our science teacher, who is also the department head, became a vegan over the summer. He told the class that there wouldn't be any dissections this year.

"We're going to do a virtual dissection of a frog instead," Mr. Brooks announced.

The kids at my lab table looked at each other and smirked.

I walked home from school and checked my e-mail... Nothing!

I texted Lily: "U got anything?"

"Nope," she replied. "GTG, taking Wonder to the groomer with my mom."

Wonder is a teacup poodle. I "wonder" how much grooming something that size actually needs.

Checked my e-mail again, and still nothing. I was getting really nervous. We had to give Ms. Lamb two outside topic suggestions by tomorrow, and we still had no input about the topics that we created.

I looked up the virtual frog. It looked almost as gross as it would have in real life. At least there wouldn't be any formaldehyde smell to deal with.

Dinner came and went with everyone in the house rather preoccupied with their own thoughts, until Mom piped up.

"So I heard on the radio that the unhealthiest Halloween candies are caramel candies, which get stuck in your teeth, and the hard sucking candies." Everyone looked at her. Then she added, "Maybe this year we should give out little bags of carrots. They're orange, a perfect Halloween color."

I was still thinking about how I hadn't heard from anyone about my project, and then I flipped out.

"Carrots for Halloween. Well, that's just great. Most of my school already thinks I'm weird. Carrots at Halloween. Now there's the perfect solution! Everyone will think, 'How cool— carrots. Wish I'd thought of that!'"

"I was kidding," Mom said. "But what do you mean that everyone thinks you're weird? What's that all about?"

"Oh, forget it!" I left the table and sulked my way upstairs.

When I got to my room, there was a text on my phone from Lily.

"Just looked again. Ton of replies. Call me."

I called her, pulled up my e-mail, and sure enough, I had about thirty e-mails of my own.

I opened the first one and read: "My biggest problem is you."

"Try the next one," said Lily.

"My biggest problem is what to wear to Taylor's party." Taylor was having a party and didn't invite me. My stomach started to hurt.

"Try the next," said Lily.

"My biggest problem is that boys hate me." This one was signed 'girl with problem.'

"Fantastic!" said Lily. "That one's on our list, so it also counts for getting a positive opinion on one of our topics."

The next e-mail problem was also on our list. And the next, and the next.

I didn't want to say that I was happy that these kids had problems, but they sure were making our lives easier.

I said, "Okay, let's go through the rest on our own and see what the different topics are. Text me when you're done. Then we'll talk."

"Okay…This is soooo exciting," Lily said.

I grunted, but felt excited as well.

9/13 - 8:00 p.m.

Scrolling through the e-mails revealed that most kids were talking about the same problems as us. After Lily called me back, we created our last two required topics.

The first was: I don't like my looks.

This topic included all personal complaints such as, *I don't like my hair, my nose, my eyes, my ears; I am too tall, too short, too fat, too skinny.*

The second topic was: My parents ask too many questions.

Why didn't I think of that?

We were done. I told Lily I'd see her tomorrow and went back online to look some more at the virtual frog.

9/14 - only Wednesday

Ugh! This feels like the longest week of my life. I just didn't feel like getting up for school again, and there are still two more days to go.

We handed in our topic results to Ms. Lamb. She looked everything over, approved the outline, and then told us one chapter is due every week. Each chapter only needs to be a few pages. That doesn't sound too bad.

We can do more than one a week if we're motivated and build in some lag time in case of writer's block. Ms. Lamb explained that writer's block occurs when you couldn't think of what to write about. Now that was something to look forward to. Let's say writer's block happened for the whole fall semester—then what?

Lily came over after school. As we were walking to my house, Taylor and Lindsay passed us with their *new* group of friends from the populars. I overheard them talking about Taylor's party. It felt awful to be on the outside with people I used to think were my best friends, but I just tried to focus on what Lily was saying.

"...and we really need to get started." She looked up, saw Taylor and Lindsay, and then looked over to me. "Let's do the

'My friends don't want to be with me' chapter first since you're having personal experience with it right now."

I looked at her. "No—I think I want to do the chapter on 'I don't know how to tell my friend that something is wrong with her.' I think I've got some clever ideas for that one."

"So we're friends?" Lily asked.

"Um, I guess, ye-ah."

"Well…okay!" Lily grabbed my arm and pulled me past the pop girls toward my block.

"Really, though, what should we start on first?" Lily asked as we sat down at the kitchen table. I'd introduced her to my mom, and we settled in.

"Let's do the 'shy one,'" I suggested. "It's not a problem we have, so it doesn't hit too close to home."

"Okay," said Lily in between mouthfuls of the apples and peanut butter that my mom set out on the table in front of us. Mom was hovering. I looked meaningfully at her, and she left.

"So what things do we know about combatting shyness?"

"Let's look on the Internet."

The Google search came up with:

20 ways to overcome shyness
8 tips on overcoming shyness
5 ways to cure shyness
10 ways to shake shyness

And about three million more results.

"I guess there are a lot of shy people out there," Lily said.

"Let's start with something like, about 50 percent of the kids in the world are shy," I said. "We've seen this on a couple of sites."

"Okay," said Lily. "Should we advertise again and get ten shy kids to tell us how they feel about things?"

"So we should do something like this?" I wrote:

> *WANTED: 10 really shy people to come and share with us all of their worst stories.*

"That should bring them running to our door," I said.

"Yeah, I guess you're right." Lily laughed.

It was nice to see that Lily didn't always take herself so seriously. I started to type:

CHAPTER ONE: Combatting Shyness

Google says that 50 percent of kids are shy. So you have a lot of company. We looked up shy people, and look who's on the list:

Lady Gaga
J. K. Rowling
Tina Fey
Brad Pitt
Emma Watson
Tom Cruise
Jim Carrey
Carrie Underwood

So maybe if you are shy, you're actually going to be famous when you grow up. In the meantime,

here are some ideas for feeling a little better
when you feel shy.

"Should we say this?" Lily asked. "Some guy named Andre
Dubus said, 'Shyness has a strange element of narcissism, a
belief that how we look, how we perform, is truly important to
other people.'"

First we looked up *narcissism*. "Narcissism," Lily read out
loud. "Excessive love or admiration of oneself."

"No!" I said. "That would just send someone under a
rug. How about this: 'Even when a girl is as shy as a mouse,
you still have to beware of the tiger within.' It's a Chinese
proverb."

Lily took over typing, adding *boy* to the proverb:

Even when a girl (or boy) is as shy as a mouse,
you still have to beware of the tiger within—
Chinese proverb.

"So now we are changing thousand-year-old quotes?" I
asked.

Lily shrugged. "Yup!" She continued:

First, there is nothing wrong with feeling shy. It
is just how you feel. It doesn't mean that you
have to be different than you are.

Second, maybe the fact that you feel shy is
because of annoying things that other people

have said. Maybe you're not that shy. Maybe it's that other people can ask silly questions like:

"Why are you so quiet?"

So if this happens, understand that they may not realize that someone doesn't have to say something all of the time. Maybe that kid just talks too much.

Lily typed this and looked up at me to see if I agreed. I thought that was pretty good.

Third, here are some things to try when you feel shy:

We looked at each other. We had no idea what to say, so we went back to the Internet and hit the jackpot with a wikiHow site on overcoming shyness.
We added some of the tips that we found:

Stand up straight—strange but true. If you stand up straight, your mind starts to think that you are more confident than you are.

If you compare yourself to others, think about how messed up they all are.

Don't worry about other people. Just because someone is popular, it doesn't mean that he or she is a happy person.

This one really surprised Lily and me.

"Hmm. I'll keep this one in mind the next time I see Taylor and Lindsay, running after those girls," I said.

> ...And remember to breathe slowly. If you slow down your breathing, your body will start to relax and you might start feeling less shy.

We wrote some more tips and stopped around dinnertime.

"I think that does it for shy," said Lily. "Plus, I have to go home and exercise Wonder."

I smiled, thinking about Wonder running on a gerbil wheel.

"Why don't you come to my house after school on Tuesday and we can start another chapter?" she asked.

"Sounds good," I said. "See you tomorrow."

Lily left, and I thought, *She's not that bad to hang out with.*

I also decided I wasn't going to spend another minute fretting about Taylor or Lindsay. I had better things to think about.

9/15 - only Thursday

I woke up, thrilled that it was finally Friday, and then realized that I was a day off. At least we had one chapter completed ahead of time. I got dressed and headed downstairs.

Audrey was already at the breakfast table along with Dad, who was finishing up his coffee and getting ready to leave for the office. Mom was getting my lunch ready. I put a waffle in the toaster and stood over it, waiting for it to pop.

"On Saturday, after soccer, we're going to visit Aunt Mimi. She's been in her new place for a month, and it's time that we stop by," Mom said.

I always loved seeing Aunt Mimi. She was my dad's aunt. She told good stories and always had chocolates.

Audrey was busy texting someone, half listening to the conversation.

"Who are you so busy texting?" I asked.

She looked at me and smiled. "It's this new guy in my class, Jake. I think that he's coming over after school."

Hmm, hmm, hmm, I thought. *Could Audrey possibly, actually have a boyfriend?* I gave her a funny look, and just as I was about to say something, Mom said, "Wonderful! I'll be home this afternoon. I look forward to meeting him."

Dad smiled and Audrey mumbled, "Great."

I left for school and ran into Lily on the way there. As we were walking, Taylor and Lins passed by, almost knocking us over in their hurry to catch up to the popular crowd they were trying so hard to be part of. Lily and I looked at each other. I knew that she was also thinking about what we wrote the day before; about how popular people weren't necessarily happy. We just smiled at each other.

One pop quiz in math, assignments for social studies, science, Spanish, more math assignments, and school finally ended for the day. I bolted home because I wanted to check out this new "friend" of Audrey's. I got home first just as Mom was parking the car. She was juggling an armful of groceries and her laptop. I grabbed a bag and helped her in.

"So how was your day?" Mom asked.

"Long and full of lots of homework." I examined the spoils of her grocery hunt, grabbed a box of cheese crackers, poured some milk, and sat down to wait for Audrey and her new friend. Mom sat down and pretended to be busy with her cellphone. She was waiting too. Fifteen minutes went by. Mom checked her watch and got up to do some chore. I pulled out my homework. After another fifteen minutes, Mom popped her head in the kitchen.

"Audrey here yet?"

"Nope." Just then we heard voices, mainly Audrey's. The door opened, and in walked Audrey with this reasonably good-looking boy.

"Guys, this is Jake."

"Hey," Jake said. Audrey handed Jake a bag of chips and grabbed two water bottles. He followed her out to the porch. Mom looked at me and winked, picked up her laptop, and started to head toward the office.

24

"She could have introduced me," I said, somewhat annoyed.

"Don't feel bad, sweetie," Mom said. "Right now he doesn't really care. He probably knows your name, since Audrey never stops talking about everything anyway." She left the room. I started on my homework since there was nothing else left to do.

About an hour later, Audrey and Jake came back into the kitchen. Jake was looking for another snack. *Man, this kid eats a lot*, I thought. I asked Jake how he liked school.

He looked at Audrey and smiled. "It's been great so far."

Blech, I thought. *He actually really likes her.* They sat down at the table and started talking about whatever, pretty much forgetting that I was there. I left the table with my stuff and went up to my room to get some more homework out of the way.

About a half hour later, I heard the outside door shut and then heard Audrey coming up the stairs. I ran out to—not sure what. She had a huge grin on her face.

"So, I guess you like him?" I asked.

"Yup."

"He sounded a little *blechy* when he said that school was great and looked at you so *meeeaningfully*," I teased.

"I guess," she said. She was too happy, so I decided to stir the pot a bit more. "I'm going to call him your *boyblech*. He's a little too mushy for me."

She looked at me and smiled, then went into her room and shut the door.

That girl is just too happy.

9/16 - Friday, Friday, Friday, Friday!!!

Happy to have the day be over. Happy that it's going to pour all weekend and there's no soccer practice tomorrow. Happy that Taylor won't have a nice day for her party and happy to be seeing Aunt Mimi tomorrow too.

9/17 - semisweet Saturday

It was awful outside. I woke up and stayed in bed, feeling very cozy. Downstairs I heard Dad rustling around in the kitchen, and I caught a whiff of something that smelled like a fantastic breakfast. I put on my comfy slippers and went downstairs. Dad was flipping his famous chocolate chip pancakes. Mom was leaning on the counter, talking to Dad about some office thing. I grabbed a stray chip and waited expectantly for a yummy pancake to show up. This had the makings of a great day.

After a delicious breakfast of pancakes and strawberries, we all got ready to go see Aunt Mimi. As we drove through the gates of her complex, I noticed the sign that read: "Welcome to Branches, An Assisted Living Facility."

"What's assisted living?"

"It's a place where people who are older, like Aunt Mimi, live when they need a little help with different chores. They find it easier to live in a place where those services are readily available," Mom said.

Audrey looked up from her book. "I didn't know that she needed so much help."

"This place has all sorts of activities, plus a dining room so Aunt Mimi doesn't have to worry about cooking, or cleaning up for that matter," said Mom.

"Maybe we should try to get into assisted living," I said. "Then we'd never have to take out the garbage again."

"Sounds like a plan," said Dad.

Mom rolled her eyes. "No such luck, you guys."

The place looked kind of cool. There were a lot of old people milling around in the lobby, and there was a café with free cookies that I noticed as we walked toward the elevator to go up to Mimi's apartment. She was on the fourth floor. On her door was this big sign that said: "Welcome Mimi Klein. We're happy to have a new neighbor."

Mimi has been here for four weeks. I guess she likes the sign. We knocked on the door and heard her walking over. She looked thrilled to see us. She gave me a big hug, and I realized that I'm almost as tall as her. This isn't such a big accomplishment, because Mimi is barely five feet tall.

"Gaby, you're going to be taller than me very soon, and you and Audrey both look so beautiful!" We smiled at her and looked around. All of Mimi's knickknacks were there. The apartment looked familiar and homey.

"So how do you like it here, Aunt Mimi?" Dad asked.

"It's pretty nice. The food is good, and there are a lot of clubs to join." Mimi hesitated. "I'm still getting used to some of the people. Let's get out of here, and I'll give you a tour." We followed her down the hall and passed a very cute old man who looked like he was checking Mimi out.

"Who is *that*?" I asked.

"Oh, that's Jack. He just moved in last week, and he's very friendly."

"How friendly is he, Aunt Mimi?" Dad teased. She ignored him and pressed the elevator button. When the doors opened, we joined three women. Mimi greeted them and introduced us.

"This is Jean, Marie, and Carol, and this is some of my family." The women seemed friendly enough. After they stepped out of the elevator, they walked toward the café. Mimi steered us in the other direction.

"But there are cookies in there, Aunt Mimi!"

She pulled us close. "Those women are so cliquey. They never invite me to join in."

"You mean there are cliques here, and people leave each other out?" I was incredulous.

"Yup—like grade school all over again. Who would think that old folks like us could be so silly? But never mind that. There are plenty of other people here, and I'll find my place. I always have, and I always will!"

I gave Aunt Mimi a hug and said, "You're pretty awesome!"

"Awesome is my middle name. Come to think of it, I *would* like a cookie and some tea." Aunt Mimi grabbed Audrey and me, and off we went to the café.

9/20 - teaming-up Tuesday

Ms. Lamb let us work in our groups today, so Lily and I got a head start on the next chapter. "Let's do the 'Girls don't like me' one," I said. "I went to visit my aunt Mimi, and she's still having trouble with girls—I mean women—too, and she's eighty-one!"

"Well, wonderful," said Lily. "It never goes away."

"At least we know that everyone, and really *everyone*, runs into this problem," I said.

CHAPTER TWO: Winning with Making Friends

Back to the Internet we went, and there was a lot to weed through. When we searched *girls don't like me*, all we got at first were a bunch of complaining boys. It was amazing how much boys had to complain about. They said things like, "I just don't have *it*," or "They don't like me because I'm too nice."

We realized that this wasn't helping us. Then we found "How to be cool and popular" on wikiHow:

Get cool clothes.

"This plays into another problem," said Lily.

Get cool electronics.

We didn't like those suggestions, so we went to another site, and then just started writing:

> It's hard to be in middle school and find that you have no friends. If you have no friends in your class, try joining something like a club or a sport that you really enjoy, and maybe you'll make some friends there.

I didn't feel particularly convinced about this sentence, and neither did Lily. We did some more Internet scouring and found some more ideas.

> You have a lot of different ways to make some new friends. Here are some good options.

> Look for a girl who is *friendable*. She doesn't have to be popular. She just has to seem nice. Think of something pleasant to say to this new person. Examples could be saying something nice to her about her clothes or asking her about her classes.

wikiHow was now proving more helpful.

> Make conversation with a lot of kids.

> Listen to what the new possible friend or friends are saying and look interested.

31

Make sure that you are not too loud or too pushy.

Think about all of the things that you like about
yourself and realize that many kids will want to
be friends with you.

We weren't convinced about what we just wrote, but we put
it on our list anyway.

If the girls around you are just too boring, maybe
there is a boy who you want to be friends with. If
all else fails, make the boy your friend.

"That sounds a little desperate," I said, looking over Lily's
shoulder.

Lily said, "Yeah, but it's a good idea anyway." She thought a
moment and then said, "Okay, how about this?" Not looking up,
she typed another suggestion from the Internet.

Offer them some gum or candy.

I was quiet for a minute, thinking about Lily's Jolly Ranchers.
"That was a really good idea."

Lily smiled at me, and we did some more Internet searches.
The best suggestion we found was:

Always surround yourself with kids who make
you feel good.

It made sense and actually should have been a no-brainer,
but I bet no one does it.

When school was over, Lily and I met and walked over to her house. I hadn't been there before and was looking forward to meeting the *wonder* dog. It was a really warm day, so we stopped to get some ice cream on the way.

"Maybe we should put a script in this chapter," I suggested. "Like a play-acting scene of what you shouldn't do if you want to make friends. That might make the chapter a little more fun. Or, how about the ten things you don't want to say or do when trying to make a new friend?"

"I like the second idea," Lily said. "Let's make a list." We sat down on Lily's stoop, finished our cones, and made a list:

> There are certain things that you may not want to do when trying to make a new friend. Here is our suggested list of things *not* to do:
>
> Don't say, "I really like you," as the first thing you say to someone. They will never talk to you again.
>
> Don't say, "I am a really boring person." They also will never talk to you again.
>
> Don't tell them everything about you without asking about them. They won't talk to you and will also hide when they see you coming.

I giggled, imagining that one.

> Don't tell them that you think something is stupid, without knowing a little more about them.

For example, saying that you think stuffed animals are dumb might really offend a stuffed-animal collector. At the least, she will never invite you over.

Don't start telling them other people's secrets. This does not build trust.

Don't keep talking on and on and on...They will fall asleep.

Try not to complain too much. People don't like to hear a lot of complaining.

Don't tell them how great you are. They won't believe you.

Don't do anything gross. We won't elaborate. If they do stay on to be your friend, you will really have to wonder whether you want to be *their* friend.

Don't leave your house without brushing your teeth and showering. You may be an extraordinary person, but no one will ever get close enough to know.

We added one more for good luck:

Don't look miserable. Remember to smile sometimes. Most people want to see a friendly face.

But don't also think that you are funnier than
you are. It will be annoying.

The list was complete. We went inside.

Lily was greeted by the smallest, yappiest dog that I had
ever seen. She put down her backpack, picked up Wonder, and
cuddled her for a bit. I leaned over to pet her, and she seemed
very happy with all of the attention. Lily waved to a woman in
the backyard.

"That's Karen. She watches my little sister in the afternoon
until my mom gets home." I assumed that she was there for Lily
also, but didn't say anything.

We went outside, and Wonder scampered behind us. Lily's
eight-year-old sister, Emily, was having a playdate. She smiled at
us and went back to talking to her friend. We sat on the porch
steps and thought about the next chapter. We were tired from the
last chapter and were actually ahead of schedule, so we decided
to hang out in the backyard.

"So have you talked to Taylor or Lindsay recently?" Lily
asked.

"No, not really, and I don't really care about them," I said.

"Oh," said Lily, looking uncomfortable.

"Why?"

"Well, um, Lindsay and Taylor are in science with me, and
they're at my lab table. So is Alexis, that girl from their 'new and
improved' group," Lily said sarcastically. She took a deep breath.
"And Alexis is saying mean things to me, and now the whole
table is starting to join in."

I felt sorry for Lily. It was bad enough that my friends had
abandoned me, but now it seemed like they were ganging up on
Lily.

"Maybe we should do the chapter on bullying next."

"Maybe," said Lily.

We heard the front door open, and in walked Lily's mom. She dropped a bunch of bags on the floor, came outside, gave Lily a huge hug, and petted Wonder, who was yapping like crazy. Giving me a wave, she said, "I'll be back," and then walked over to Emily and Karen. Emily ran to her mom and started gabbing about her day and her after-school snack. She asked her mom to play hide-and-seek with her and her friend. Lily's mom smiled and said, "Maybe later," and came back to sit with Lily and me.

"Hi, you must be Gaby. I'm Ellen," she said. "Lily has said a lot about you." Lily did the "oh mom" thing, and her mom asked me if I wanted to stay for dinner. Before I could answer, her cell phone started vibrating. She looked down and said, "How nice—text messages from Groupon and my pedometer app—my two best friends." She looked back at me. "Check with your mom or dad. I can drive you home after dinner." She got up and walked back into the house.

"If you want to stay, that would be great. We could do our homework together and hang out," Lily added.

I texted my mom. She came back in a few minutes with "Sure." We went into the kitchen and pulled out our homework. I didn't say anything more to Lily about her lab table and was glad that she was thinking about something else.

Within a few minutes, I heard a *stomp, stomp, stomp* in the next room. I looked up and saw Lily's mom marching back and forth, staring at her phone. "She's using the pedometer app and playing some word game at the same time," Lily said.

"She just walks back and forth?" I asked.

"Yup!" Ellen yelled. "It feels like forever, but it's only for about forty minutes." Wonder yapped and followed her back and forth until the little dog was wiped out. We turned back to our homework. After a while Emily and her friend came inside, and Lily and I went upstairs.

Ellen is a decorator, and Lily's house shows it. Everything in the living room is red, black, and white. The red buttons and throw pillows on the black sofa both perfectly match the carpet. The black sofa looks really nice with the red pillows. We went upstairs to Lily's room, and it was just as stylish. She and her sister have this white furniture in their rooms with this really flowery wallpaper and cozy pastel rugs, and the throw pillows match the wallpaper exactly. I thought about my house, where things are comfortable but more thrown together.

Lily's mom popped her head into the room. She was a little red in the face. "Dad will be home late. Emily's friend Janie is staying for dinner too, so it will just be us girls." She bounced out of the room with Wonder, Emily and her playdate following close behind. Lily and I finished up our homework while we chatted back and forth.

Dinner was really fun. We had spaghetti and meatballs (one of my favorites) and veggie sticks. Emily and Janie jabbered on about their days. Lily's family plays a game at dinner called "And guess what happened next." They each talk about something that happened in their day and stop at a part where everyone else has to guess what happened next. Emily and Janie were very excited to play.

Emily began. "So Joey, in our class, brought in this ant farm that he has at home." Janie started to laugh. "Guess what happened next?"

We all knew, and just as I was about to say something, Ellen jumped in. "All the ants ate ice cream with spoons for snack!"

"No!" yelled Janie.

Lily said, "All the ants danced to the *Happy* song!"

"You know that they didn't do that," said Emily in an annoyed but still amused voice.

"Oh, but it was possible that the ants ate ice cream with spoons?" Lily asked, with a smile on her face.

"Okay, what happened?" asked Lily's mom.

At the same time, the little girls yelled, "The ant farm fell over, and the ants got out, and there were ants everywhere!"

"Sounds like a wild day in second grade," said Lily.

"Okay. Lily, do you want to go next?" her mom asked.

Lily looked down and then glanced at the little girls. "No, not right now."

Lily's mom said to Emily and Janie, "I think there's something good on TV right now. Why don't you and Janie go see?" They ran out of the room.

Ellen started to clear some of the dinner plates and asked, "So, how was your day?"

Lily looked at me and said, "Well, Gaby already knows. So… some girls are being kind of mean in lab. They're ganging up on me. I'll see if it gets better, but if it doesn't, I'm not sure what to do."

I was really surprised that Lily was being so open about this, in front of me and her mom. It was interesting that she wasn't worried about being a tattletale or a baby.

Lily's mom said, "Well, we've talked about this before. The world is different for kids and adults. If an adult is made to feel uncomfortable by other adults, they have different options. If it's really bad, they can call the police and sometimes there are consequences. Adults aren't called tattletales for trying to keep themselves comfortable, so why should kids be labeled? The rules should be the same."

"You mean call the police?" I blurted out.

"No, not call the police, but you should realize there is nothing, and I mean nothing, wrong with sticking up for yourself. You could tell a teacher or a guidance counselor, make sure your parents know right away, or tell the kid really loudly in that moment to keep their mouth shut. If a teacher hears you, the problem may be addressed right then and there. You may get in trouble for talking out loud, but the problem will also be out there, and the attention will now be on the bully. The last thing that kid wants is to get in trouble. And definitely do not keep it to yourself. It's not your fault that someone else is rude and nasty. The sooner it's stopped, the better."

Lily smiled, looking mischievous. "I can't wait for tomorrow."

Her mom said, "Go for it, honey."

Lily was quite chipper on the car ride to my house. I thanked Ellen for the lift and for dinner. I went inside, watched some TV, got ready for bed, and thought about the dinner conversation. I had never heard a mom encouraging her kid to yell at someone in class. It was kind of revolutionary. I never thought that a mom would be willing to tell her kid to get in trouble with the teacher, but it made sense. Why sit there and take it? It would be interesting to see what happened.

I went downstairs. Audrey was still doing some homework in the kitchen, and Mom and Dad were chatting about something. I announced, "I just want to let you know that there may be a day that I'll yell at someone in school, and if I do, it will be for a great reason, and I may get in trouble with the teacher, and she or he may call you!" I stopped to catch my breath and looked at them all.

Audrey looked back. "Well, okay!"

I left the room, and as I walked upstairs, I heard Dad ask Mom, "What did they feed her over there?"

I yelled down, "Spaghetti, and it was delicious!" And then I went to my room.

9/21 - whoa-Lily Wednesday

Math is killing me. I am going to die from math poisoning. I mean it. It isn't just that there are tons of math problems due every week. It's that some of the word problems are ridiculous. Other ones, like distance problems, confuse me. For example:

> Two cyclists start at the same time from opposite ends of a course that is 45 miles long. One cyclist is riding at 14 mph, and the second cyclist is riding at 16 mph. How long after they begin will they meet?

I never remember where to start, and I'm always more interested in what kind of day it was when they were cycling, where the cyclists live, and so on.

When my first math quiz came back and I saw that I had failed it, I stuffed it in my backpack and tried to think about something else. Ms. Farrell wrote a note that I should see her after class, and also said that my parents needed to sign the quiz. (It wasn't just me—everyone's parents had to.)

When class ended I stayed to speak with her. A lot of other kids—like half the class—were also there. At least I wasn't alone, but it was really embarrassing to be a failure.

Ms. Farrell said to us, "I know that this test was hard, so I'm giving you a few extra problems of this type in addition to your homework to practice this week at home. Please hand them in on Monday." I sighed and grabbed the worksheet, stuck it in my folder, and marched on to science class.

I waved to Lily, who was entering the classroom next to mine. Today was the day that we were supposed to start the virtual frog project. We were all seated with our lab partners at our tables, and each team shared an iPad. The teacher started to explain how we would start, when all of a sudden I heard from the other room:

"Alexis! Don't you dare say those mean things to me. You are a really rude person."

Well, it was certainly loud, and it was certainly Lily. As everyone in our class tried very hard to listen to what was going on in the next room, the door opened, and we heard the teacher send both Lily and Alexis to the assistant principal. I saw Lily walk out with a huge smile on her face and Alexis looking downcast. Mr. Brooks tried to settle down the class and had us start the project.

We were busy answering questions on the iPad and pointing out different parts of the frog's anatomy when I saw Lily and Alexis march back into their classroom, accompanied by the assistant principal, Ms. Alt. Our class started whispering again. Mr. Brooks shushed us and shut the door. I couldn't wait for lunch.

Lily was a few minutes late leaving science. I waited outside my classroom, pretending to look busy. First Alexis walked out, and a few minutes later Lily followed, looking pretty smug.

"What happened?" I asked.

"Well," she said, "we sat outside the office and waited for Ms. Alt. She called me in and then called my mom and put her on speaker. My mom said that although I shouldn't yell in class for no reason, she would be happier to not have someone bothering her daughter, and sometimes yelling is what is needed. Ms. Alt had me go sit outside and brought Alexis into her office and shut the door. I heard everything they said. She called Alexis's mom, who said that she and Alexis would discuss this further at home. Ms. Alt said something like 'see you at your next emotional intelligence committee meeting' and got off the phone. She came out with Alexis, and we went back to class. Ms. Garcia moved Alexis's seat away from her friends and put this very quiet, nice girl, Amy, next to me. Not a bad for day's work!"

"Sounds pretty good to me," I said.

The cafeteria was buzzing. We sat down, and a few kids came by to tell Lily that they were sick of Alexis and her friends, and that they had heard about Lily yelling and were thinking about trying it themselves sometime. Amy and two of her friends, Sara and Imani, came to sit with Lily and me. We had a really nice time at lunch. At recess, Lily got a lot of "heys" and smiles.

"I'm famous," Lily said to me, jokingly. We went to class, ready to start our next chapter on bullying.

CHAPTER THREE: Beating the Bully and the "Cy-bore" (boring kids on the Internet with nothing better to do than) Bully

"Sounds a little violent, don't you think? And what's with the cy-bore bully thing?" I asked Lily, looking over her shoulder. We were back in our groups using laptops for the project. We had a double period of language arts, so we had a lot of time to work on our chapter.

"Let's leave it for now—I'm still enjoying my morning victory! We received a lot of e-mail about bullying and about kids getting bullied on the Internet. Let's make the cyber bullies as boring as possible."

> At one time or another, everyone is bothered by someone else, but no one should ever be bullied, and the bully is never right.

We paused, stared blankly at each other, and then went back to the Internet to figure out what to write next.

"Wow! It says here that three-quarters of kids say that they have been bullied at one time or another," I said. "That means that either one-quarter of the kids are doing all of the bullying, or that some kids who get bullied have done some bullying too."

"I know that I once bullied someone when I was little, and their mom scolded me and then told my mom," said Lily. "And my mom said that the other mom was right to talk to me and say stop!" I was getting confused with all of the moms in that story, but one thing did stand out. Sometimes moms or dads really need to get involved. So I typed:

> It's important to get other people involved. Sometimes you just can't handle something on your own. Asking for help doesn't make you a baby. It shows confidence when you ask for help and talk about the problem.

I looked up at Lily, and she was beaming. She grabbed the laptop and continued.

> Steps for dealing with a bully:
> If someone bothers you once, give them another chance and hope they won't bother you again, but hope for the best and prepare for the worst.

Lily was busy typing. "Where did that come from?" I asked. "I dunno—my dad says this a lot, and it sounds right here." "I have no idea what that means." "It means that...Here, wait." Lily typed some more.

> This means that, maybe the bully had a bad day last time and they realized on their own that they should behave differently. But just in case they bother you again, have a plan. Do not wait for a third time. Every time a bully bullies and you do nothing, the bully just gets stronger.

So now Lily stopped, and we tried to figure out some steps. Back to the Internet and the two million-plus search results.

"Look at this," Lily said. "Here is one on how to deal with bullies in the workplace." She looked stunned, and I felt the same. "Another problem that even grown-ups have sometimes. You'd think these problems would go away when you grow up, but they just seem to reappear!"

> Believe it or not, we saw on the Internet that there are also "workplace bullies," so the sooner

you figure out how to deal with this stuff the better.

First, never let the bully get to you. The more the bully knows that they are bothering you, the more they will continue to do so.

Never blame yourself for being bullied. It is *never* your fault. It is always the bully's fault.

Have witnesses who can defend your version of what happened and what the bully said.

"Or create a bunch of witnesses by yelling real loud in class and accusing the bully in public in front of the teacher and your classmates," I joked. Lily thought and typed.

Don't be afraid to speak up for yourself even if you are loud and are in a quiet place.

Don't put the bully down. Instead, tell the bully that they are really too smart to be saying such stupid, mean things.

See if there is a "bully box" at school where you can drop a note or on the school website where you can send an e-mail. A guidance counselor or teacher will follow up on the problem.

We didn't have a bully box e-mail site at school, but we thought that this was a pretty good idea. We also remembered that we had received a couple of e-mails from kids who said they had a problem with a bully. "Let's send them e-mails saying what you did, Lily, and also tell them to make sure that they tell someone. It's lonely to stay bullied."

"Sounds good," she said. She continued to type:

> Ignore the bully. Don't let them know that they are getting to you.
>
> If you see someone getting bullied:
>
> *   Don't join in.
>
> *   Realize that doing nothing to stop the bully means that you are doing something. It means that you agree with what is happening. It makes the bully think that you agree with them. It makes the person being bullied think that they are even more alone.
>
> *   Try to change the subject and talk about something else to give the bully something else to think about.
>
> *   Speak up for the person who is feeling bullied, if you feel that you can do this. It takes a lot of courage to stand up to a bully.
>
> *   Encourage the kid being bullied to tell a teacher or their parents.

We caught our breath, and Lily asked, "Wouldn't it be great if whenever someone texted or wrote something mean online, a giant hammer came out from the screen, like Whack-A-Mole, and clopped them on the head?" I felt immediately inspired and continued typing.

> Then, if public bullies aren't bad enough, there are the cyber—or as we like to call them, "cy-bore"—bullies who hide on the Internet, or in text world, and have nothing better to do with their time than to be annoying and obnoxious by keyboard. These kids must have such boring lives of their own that they need to do some-thing to keep themselves busy. They can be very hurtful. Here are some additional steps to deal with the cy-bore(s). Some of these steps are the same for beating the bully. wikiHow and kidshealth.org have some great ideas.
>
> * Tell someone. Just as with in-person bullying, it is important to tell an adult right away.
>
> * Walk away from your electronics! Do not respond. Do not forward the text to a friend. Go do something you enjoy so you don't have to focus on the nastiness. Later when you are calmer, you can think of your next steps.
>
> * Save all of the bullying evidence. Write the date and time of the bullying. It may be that

this person can get in legal or school trouble, or even Internet trouble, for their comments.

* Report the cy-bore. If you need help with this, get your parent or a trusted adult involved. Places like Facebook and YouTube and phone-service providers take bullying through their services very seriously, and the bully could wind up losing access to the sites or phone service.

* In general, never discuss anything personal that may be embarrassing online or in texts. Save that for private phone calls or when you're in person.

"Losing Internet and phone service sounds pretty terrifying, and also like a great revenge tool," I said.

If your friends are teasing someone online or by text:

* Do not get involved in the bullying, but get involved by telling an adult that cyberbullying is happening to someone you know.

* If you feel you can, let the cyber bully know that cyberbullying is just as bad as bullying in person.

*   Never forward any mean photos or texts that you get that are about someone else. Just because you didn't start the bullying doesn't mean that you aren't part of the problem, and you can get in trouble.

We were pretty much done, so with the time we had left, I started on my miserable math problems.

9/27 - tamed Tuesday

It's been a couple of easy days. School was okay. Soccer was okay. Audrey still has that boyblech, and Lily and I sat with Amy, Imani, and Sara at lunch again. Alexis seemed to be real quiet. Lily told me that the night after the assistant principal visit, Alexis called her and apologized. "I know that her mom made her call, but who cares? It felt good."

We also e-mailed a few notes back to the kids who had said they were bullied, and yesterday there was shouting in two classrooms, one in the morning and one in the afternoon. The shouting sounded an awful lot like Lily's. And then we heard about some more trips to Ms. Alt's office. Lily got a few more "heys" and smiles, and the principal made an announcement that we would be having an assembly about bullying.

I came home with a lot of homework and needed to study for my next math quiz. I pulled out the practice worksheet that Ms. Farrell gave us, looked it over, and started to panic. I needed to calm down so I left everything on the table and took Scout out for a walk. The sky was turning pretty gray, and it was getting windy. I really didn't want to study for the quiz. I really hate everything that has to do with math. I really don't want to fail another quiz.

As soon as Scout was finished with her business, I led her back into the house, sat at the kitchen table and started to cry.

"'S'up?" asked Audrey. I hadn't realized she was downstairs. She usually hangs around on Tuesday afternoons until my mom gets home from work. I guess she's my unofficial sitter.

I said, "Nothing—leave me alone!"

"Oh, come on," she said. She glanced down at my math worksheet and picked it up. "Oh cool! I love distance problems!"

I looked at her with deep hatred. I started to say something but it just turned into more crying. She sat down calmly and looked at me. "Someone is having a math meltdown. I think that you need...*drumroll*!" She beat her hands on the table. "The Math Therapist."

Now I was really concerned that she was crazy. I also had absolutely no idea what she was talking about.

"What?" I gulped.

"Let me help you *dahling*," Audrey said. "I know I can. I've helped many others before you—well maybe one or two. But you can be helped, and you can triumph!"

I was so tired from crying that I just surrendered. "Okay. What do you want me to do?"

It had started to rain pretty hard outside and was gusty. *Raining outside and misery on the inside*, I thought.

"First, I want you to calm down; get a glass of water. Just relax and breathe," she said.

"Do you want me to lie down on the couch so you can analyze me too?"

"Maybe later," she said. "But right now let me look over your stuff."

It was cozy in the kitchen with Audrey. I liked the newfound attention.

"Distance problems…are like solving a mystery!" she started. I stiffened.

"Too soon?" she asked.

I nodded.

"Okay. Take a minute or two more, but we will have to start, or we can't finish!"

This was strange logic, but worth a little more stalling. I put my head down and relaxed a little. Audrey looked over the problem sheet a little more. "Ready now?"

I nodded.

"Okay!" she said. "Distance problems are like solving a mystery."

"You said that already."

Audrey looked very serious. "Are you ready to solve some mysteries?"

This girls is nuts, I thought. But I said, "Okay."

"The key to a distance problem is to identify the *one*, and there is only *one* piece of information that is missing!" She was being a little dramatic, but I got what she meant.

"So distance is equal to rate multiplied by time. D equals R times T! Do you understand this?" She was on a tear, and I was speechless. "So distance—how far you go—is equal to how fast you go times how long it takes. So get up!" I got up. She was too obsessed to ignore. "Walk across the kitchen!" she ordered. I did. "So what's the distance?" she asked. I paused. "Come on, Gaby," she said gently.

"It's the length of the kitchen?" I asked.

She gave a brisk nod. "What's the rate?"

"It's how fast I am going, right?"

"Exactly!" she said. "What's the time?"

"It's how long it took me to cross the kitchen!"

She nodded and I smiled, happy to get three answers right in a row.

"Every distance problem is about this, and nothing more. You'll know two variables and have to figure out the third. Now let's go to the mattresses!"

"Huh?" I said.

"Never mind…It means let's start and let's fight," Audrey said. "Okay. So here's the formula." She wrote $D=R*T$. "Tell me everything that you know about this formula."

"I know that it's stupid," I said.

"How's that going to work for you on the quiz?" she asked.

"Okay, okay…I know that D over R equals T, and D over T equals R," I said quickly.

"Then you know everything," she said.

We went through a bunch of problems. I identified what each part was and which part was missing, and then I solved them all. After about an hour, we stopped and took a snack break. It was five, and Mom called and said she would be home by six.

I looked at Audrey, said a quiet "thank you," and went over to hug her.

She hugged me back. "Just remember to tell yourself one thing. That thing is, 'I can do this.' Tell yourself this over and over and believe it. If you tell yourself this, you'll be able to solve those 'stupid' problems. Let me know if you need more math therapy." She smiled. "I'll be happy to give you some more if you need it."

Sometimes even your sister can be your best friend.

10/4 - telling Tuesday

Having finished "Beating the Bully and the Cy-bore Bully," Lily and I debated what to do next. We actually didn't want to do anything at all, so we just stared at each other during writing time and tried to look busy for one or two classes. That all stopped when we started giggling too much over this animal game we were playing. It's when you fold a paper in half and draw the bottoms of animals, and the other person draws the heads, without seeing the bottom. We opened the paper and decided who we should name each new animal after. We got a little too carried away with a combination cat head and octopus body and a combination mouse head and bee body, and we started naming them all after science teachers.

Ms. Lamb heard the giggling and sternly said, "Anyone who hasn't started their next chapter will need to stay late today." That was enough motivation right there.

"Okay!" I said. "What about this? We just wrote the 'Beating the bully' chapter. Let's do the 'I don't like myself' chapter and call it 'Beating yourself up—stop!'"

Lily said, "Yeah, okay, but like what exactly do you mean?"

"I mean this. So let's say that not liking yourself is actually like bullying yourself, but there are no witnesses, so you have to figure out how to protect yourself from *yourself*!"

"A little loud, Gaby...and a little dramatic. But not bad," said Lily, and she started typing.

CHAPTER FOUR: Beating Yourself Up—Stop!

> I don't like your nose. I don't like your eyes. I don't like your hair. I don't like your stomach. I don't like...

> Would you want to spend time with anyone who said these things to you? Well, why are you always saying these things to yourself?

Lily looked up from typing. I liked it, and I nodded for her to keep going.

> Self-bullying, which is what this is, is as bad as being bullied by others. So stop.

Then she stopped typing. "Are we done with this chapter?"

"I wish. So, why would you pick on yourself?"

"Well, I never do, because I'm perfect!"

"Mmn, not so much."

"Well, thanks a lot," Lily said. "You're supposed to agree with me!"

Silence followed, and we both thought some more.

I started. "I know that when I see all of those magazines with all of those great-looking models or those great-looking actresses on TV wearing all of those great-looking clothes, I run to the great-looking mirror and hope to see something as great. Well, that never happens."

"Wouldn't it be great to look like Katniss Everdeen?" We looked up Jennifer Lawrence and found out that she had been twenty-one when she played sixteen-year-old Katniss in the first *Hunger Games* movie. We looked up another actor, and found he was sixteen when he played an eighth-grader!

"Audrey once said that Rachel in *Glee* was born in 1994, meaning she was fourteen or fifteen in the show, but the actress who played her, Lea Michele, was twenty-one in real life. Audrey thought that it was silly to have someone who is twenty-one playing a fourteen- or fifteen-year-old."

"Let's make a list of other actors' and actresses' ages and the ages of the characters they played," Lily said.

It was really hard keeping the real names, fake names, real ages, and fake ages straight, but we finally had something for the chapter.

If you think that there is something wrong with the way you look, or if you think you should look a certain way, maybe you are comparing yourself to the wrong people. Maybe you are comparing yourself to actors or actresses who are much older than you think. Here is a list of some actors and actresses and how old they were when they played certain roles:

Shailene Woodley was twenty-one when she played sixteen-year-old Beatrice "Trice" Prior in *Divergent*.

Rachel McAdams was twenty-six when she played sixteen-year-old Regina George in *Mean Girls*.

Mark Salling was twenty-seven when he played fifteen-year-old Noah Puck in *Glee*.

"It seems like most of the cast of *Glee* was really in their twenties when they were supposed to be teens," Lily commented.

Robert Pattinson was twenty-six when he played someone who was supposed to be seventeen (but was actually 107) in *Twilight*.

"Do we understand that one?" I asked.

"Yes. Vampires are always way older than they look," Lily said quickly and continued typing.

Alan Ruck was thirty years old when he played a seventeen-year-old in *Ferris Bueller's Day Off*.

Monique Colman was twenty-six years old when she played a sixteen-year-old in *High School Musical*.

Amber Tamblin was twenty-two years old when she played a fifteen-year-old in *Sisterhood of the Traveling Pants*.

Tobey Maguire was twenty-six years old when he played seventeen-year-old Peter Parker in *Spiderman*.

Katie Leclerc was twenty-five years old when she played sixteen-year-old Daphne Paloma Vasquez on *Switched at Birth*.

"We need to stop and move on with the chapter," Lily said.

"Yeah, but this is way more fun than writing the book!" I said, stalling, and continued adding to the list.

Olivia Newton-John was thirty when she played seventeen-year-old Sandy in *Grease*.

Jason Earles was thirty-two when he played seventeen-year-old Jackson Stewart in *Hannah Montana: The Movie*.

Shirley Hendersen was thirty-seven years old when she played fourteen-year-old Moaning Myrtle in *Harry Potter and the Chamber of Secrets*.

"It's like an epidemic. All of these older people are playing our parts. No wonder we have no idea what we're supposed to look like…and boys too," I said.

"I would really like to see what these people looked like when they were our age," said Lily. She pulled up a picture of Lea Michele when she was twelve, and she looked young just like us, maybe even a little younger. Lily typed:

> We guess that "act your own age" doesn't really happen in showbiz, and showbiz is not real life. We are all so busy trying to look like the fifteen-year-olds that we see in the movies or on TV, but those actors could be in their twenties. They could be really, really old. Some of them could be as old as, or older than, our teachers.
>
> So now that you know that you don't have to look any different than you do, here are some additional things to think about.
>
> When you look in the mirror, before you start to think bad things about yourself, try looking yourself in the eye and saying something that you think is nice about yourself.
>
> Don't think that anyone else is perfect. No one is.

Class ended. At least we wouldn't have to stay late after school.

10/19 - whaaat? Wednesday

Strange things are happening. Lily is not the most unpopular girl in the grade anymore. We always sit with a tableful of girls now, and even sometimes boys. Amy, Imani, and Sara are regulars, and so are a few different kids on different days. Lily's bag is not full of candy anymore. Sometimes she doesn't bring any candy to school. The frog parts are virtually coming out of the frog. And I—*drumroll*—am doing pretty well in math. We've handed in the first four chapters of our book and are waiting for comments, so nothing's been due this week.

I also have this new bunch of friends. Every morning I walk to school and hang out outside or in the gym with Lily, Amy, Imani, and Sara (LAIS) until the bell rings. Then I walk with LAISG—you know, all of us—until we go to our separate classes. Then LAISG has lunch. LAISG hangs out for recess. LAISG talks in front of our lockers. LAISG stands outside school at the end of the day, until LAISG splits up to go home or to after-school clubs.

After school on Wednesday Amy, Imani, and Sara stayed late for book club. As we walked toward home, Lily and I got a group text message for LAISG: "Let's all go to the fundraiser this weekend together. Can u?"

Lily looked at me and said in amazement, "OMG!"

"What?" I asked.

"We're actually in a clique!"

"No, we aren't! We're in a group that no one else wants to be in," I said.

"No," she said. "The signs are all there. We spend all of our time with Amy, Imani, and Sara. Yesterday when Amanda came over to talk to us, she couldn't get a word in, and she walked away. We were telling mean stories about Taylor and Alexis at lunch. Later, LAISG got up and walked to a different bench at recess when those three girls sat down, and..."

"And what?" I asked.

"I can't think of anything else," she said.

I thought this over a little. We didn't have names anymore; we'd become an acronym. That was what Audrey said yesterday when I mentioned LAISG. She explained that an acronym was a short way of expressing an organization's name like UNICEF or NASA, or like saying "ASAP." And in our case, it was a shortened way of lumping five girls into one. She'd said, "Gaby, too bad your name isn't Zelda; then you could be LAISZ. Get it... *laaa-zee!*" Audrey had thought that was hysterical.

We did hang out a lot together, but it was so nice to finally have a group of people to be with. We did ignore Amanda, but she was really whiney sometimes. We did—

"You're right! We *are* becoming a clique," I said.

"Isn't it fantastic!" said Lily.

"Well, it isn't supposed to be, but it is kind of cool," I said.

"Yeah, we're like *Mean Girls*," Lily said, looking quite pleased about the whole thing.

"Not exactly. You probably mean *Sort of Mean, Sort of Teens*," I said, joking around.

"Well, we'll try to be a little bit friendlier as a group, but we'll still do a bunch of stuff together. Like I think I want to have a Halloween slumber party with LAISG. What do you think?"

"Cool," I said. "You know, since we're living it—or since we *think* we're living it—let's do the next chapter on cliques. We'll combine it with the 'My friends don't want to be with me' chapter."

Since I've recovered from the Taylor and Lindsay expulsion and since we both feel like we've got a sense of what both sides of the clique coin feel like, doing this chapter next sounded like a good idea.

"Let's see what Ms. Lamb has to say about our chapters so far, and then we'll see if we're doing this whole thing right," I said. "And now let's forget about all this stuff. See you tomorrow."

10/20 - tough-luck Thursday

The only good thing—well, maybe one of the only good things—about today is that it's almost Friday. I have so much homework it feels like it's coming out of my eyeballs!

We had our book meeting and a big debate with Ms. Lamb. She suggested that we should be using "he or she" and "her or him" instead of "they" and "them" every time we gave advice in the book. We felt that doing this would make those sentences sound awkward (and be really annoying to read, but we didn't say that to her). I then suggested making up the new catch all words *heshe* and *herhim*. Ms. Lamb looked amused, and then said that she would accept "they" and "them" in our book.

I thought everything was perfect. Then Ms. Lamb said that although she liked how we were progressing, and that all of our research up to this point was fine, the next chapters had to include something more than Google or wikiHow references. When we asked like what, she told us that some first-person interviews would be a good idea. Before she left our table, she said with a smile, "You know, twenty-seven-year-olds don't look like fifteen-year-olds, but we're not *that* old!" Then she left our table, probably thinking we enjoyed the joke, but at that moment I don't think either of us saw any humor in it.

"Great!" I said. "We have to talk to people." Lily was quiet—unusual for her. Then I had a brainstorm. "Can you sleep over tomorrow night? Audrey is having a bunch of friends over to get ready for the fundraiser bake sale this weekend, and we can ask them about cliques."

"That's a great idea!" Lily said. "Do you think that she'll mind having us around?"

"Probably...but we'll find a way to make ourselves useful, and her friends think that I'm adorable. Well, not adorable but cute enough." I gave Lily my cute face.

She didn't seem impressed, but she did say she was looking forward to a possible sleepover. So the other good thing about today is that Lily might be able to hang out tomorrow night, and if we're lucky, we can sample some cupcakes and get some juicy quotes about cliques. Friday is looking better.

Lily texted me this evening to tell me that she could sleep over. That's great, except for one thing. I'd forgotten to ask my mom. I walked into the kitchen. My mom and Audrey were going over a shopping list of ingredients that they would be picking up tomorrow for the baking party.

"Mom, is it okay if Lily sleeps over tomorrow night?"

"I have this big thing going on here tomorrow!" Audrey snapped.

Mom said, "Sure." I could tell she was happy that I was making plans, after not doing much in September.

"And you guys need to stay out of the way!" Audrey continued to snarl.

"Oh, we will." I lied. "We definitely will."

Audrey started, "You better keep—"

"They'll be fine," Mom interrupted. "If they happen to be around, you'll deal with it."

Yes! I thought, having known full well that's what my mom would say. I ran back upstairs and texted Lily a smiley face.

10/21 - favors Friday

It's finally Friday, and I had some amazing luck this morning. I was trying to figure out how to ask Audrey if she and her friends could help us with our book chapter, and then at breakfast something great happened.

"Shoot!" Audrey said, after checking a text, "I completely forgot that I need to stay late at school for this chem lab. I won't be able to get to the store with Mom to buy all of the stuff for the baking thing tonight...Gaby, is there any way that you can help her?"

The wheels of negotiation were already spinning in my head. "We-ell..." I paused for effect. "I guess I could, but I need a favor."

Audrey knew she was stuck. "Okay, what?"

"You know this book project I'm doing with Lily on middle school problems? We need to interview people about cliques. Do you think we could talk to you and your friends tonight to get some quotes?"

Audrey looked intrigued. "Sure. That's easy. But let's get the baking out of the way first, and then you can hang with us and talk."

"Great!" I said. "I'll tell Mom that I'll take your place for shopping."

I ran up to tell Mom, who was still getting ready to go to the office. A small secret: I love shopping for supplies—any kind, anywhere. I particularly love shopping for baking supplies. All of those frostings and decorations and ingredients. Just love it. I've never shared this because I was always embarrassed about it, but now it's my secret weapon!

"So Mom, I'm going to help out with the baking shopping, because Audrey forgot that she has to stay late for a science lab."

"What did it cost her?" Mom teased.

"Oh, not too much. Lily and I get to hang out with Audrey and her friends after baking to interview them for the book project."

"Sounds like a good deal all around," she said.

Mom picked me up after school, and we went to the super-market. Lily would be coming over later for dinner and the interrogation.

Audrey's list was quite long. I threw into the cart cake mixes, frostings, eggs, oil, butter, cupcake holders, coconut, chocolate chips, butterscotch chips, condensed milk, graham crackers, walnuts, marshmallows, and Rice Krispies. Then it was over to the candy section for gummy bears, M&Ms, and Reese's Pieces for decorations. I was having a blast. Mom had started to ask me about school stuff but realized pretty quickly that she was no match for the world of baking supplies.

When we returned home, I set everything out on the counter. Cupcake staples in one corner, magic bar supplies in another, and Rice Krispies treat ingredients in a third spot. I surveyed the organization plan, was satisfied, and went to relax for a while until Lily arrived.

Lily, Audrey, and her friends all converged at our house within five minutes of each other. Lily and I took her stuff upstairs, and I explained the plan.

"We lie low until Audrey and her friends are done with their baking, and then we can ask them some questions about their experiences with cliques."

We heard a lot of chat downstairs about the baking and other high school topics like who was dating whom, who was breaking up with whom, midsemester test results, the PSATs—a precollege test I wish I'd never have to think about, but I know my time is coming—and other stuff. In a little while, I smelled buttery and marshmallow smells. By 7:30, the baking was done, pizzas were delivered, and Lily and I went downstairs with a laptop, pens, and a smartphone for recording. Dad and Mom grabbed slices and drinks and went into the den.

At the dining table, serving pizza and drinks were Audrey, Jake, Nya, Camilla, Mattie, and Seth. I got greetings from the boys and some hugs from the girls, and I introduced Lily.

So Jake is still tolerating Audrey. Interesting. I also wondered, what could boys possibly have to say on the subject of cliques? Finding out would be an added plus.

We sat with the bakers and munched on pizza, waiting for an opening. Finally, after her second slice, Audrey said, "So guys, I told you that my sister and her friend have this book project that they're working on, and they need some stories about cliques."

Surprisingly, it was Seth who went first. "Okay, well, I have one. Last year my brother had a group of friends from the baseball team. His best friend, I'll call him 'T,' was not on the team, but always hung around with my brother and became part of the group. Some guy in the group decided that he didn't want 'T' to join in, so they froze him out."

"What did your brother do?" I had *so* not been expecting to be dealing with a boy situation that I wasn't taking any notes. Neither was Lily.

Seth answered. "He hung with the group and spent less time with his friend, until one day the group started to freeze *him* out. He realized how it felt and went back to his friend, apologized, and starting hanging out with his friend's new group. The guys from the baseball team started being welcoming again, and my brother stayed friendly with them, but he never bailed on 'T' after that. My brother also told me to really know who your friends are."

Then Jake jumped in. "My older brother Morgan went to junior prom last year with his girlfriend Isabella, who was from another school. He was in a group of guys who pretty much were all going with a group of girls from the popular clique in school."

"I know who you mean," said Mattie, and she rolled her eyes.

Jake continued, "That group of girls decided that if my brother was taking someone who wasn't in their group, then they couldn't be part of their limo ride. The guys all acted helpless, so my brother and Isabella went on their own. They had a great time, and my brother decided that although he would still hang out with his friends, he would cut back on the time when those girls were around."

"You know, it doesn't sound like it was only the girls who were the problem. Those guys didn't speak up, and they should have," Camilla said.

"Yeah, I guess," said Jake.

"So listen to this!" Mattie said, leaning in. "My aunt was a sub in the middle school, and she told me that even some of the teachers are in their own cliques. When she would go into the staff lunchroom, there was a 'queen bee' teacher who always had the same four other teachers around her. When my aunt sat down with them, they acknowledged her but immediately went into some conversation topic that she didn't know anything about, and no one bothered to clue her in. The next day my aunt sat with a different group, who pretty much said that those teachers were acting like they were in high school all over again!"

Audrey and her friends put away leftovers, and brought out some cupcakes to frost and decorate. Mattie took a cupcake, started frosting, and said, "I was left out by my friends when I started high school. I wasn't cool enough for them. I was busy with lacrosse and they weren't, and they didn't think I was around enough, so they actually voted me out of the group. That's when I became really good friends with Audrey and this crew." She waved a semidecorated cupcake in the direction of the high schoolers. "I traded up!" She looked around and smiled, and then said to Lily and me, "Do you guys want to help decorate?"

I looked at Audrey, who realized that there was nothing to be gained by leaving us out and the decorating and packing would go a lot faster with two more sets of hands.

Jake chimed in. "They can help me put these bars in bags." The boyblech was surprisingly pleasant. I could sort of understand why Audrey liked him. We stopped interviewing and started helping out.

After a few minutes of gummy bear placement, Lily, who had been unusually shy, piped up with a question. "So what do you do when you have to deal with cliques?"

Nya said, "I won't spend time with people who tell me who I can or can't spend time with."

Camilla added, "I also stay away from kids who make fun of other kids online. If they're so nasty, I don't want to be on their radar. Who wants to be around them anyway?"

Audrey then said, "I try to be around people who are easygoing about others joining in. That way you get to meet more people."

I was about to say, *Well, you could let* me *join in more*, but realized that I'd better not look any gift horses in the mouth. This was a favorite saying of Dad's, who loved the origin of the expression. It meant that in the old days—even before Dad's time—when you received a horse as a gift, you accepted it and didn't look in the horse's mouth to make sure that the teeth weren't rotten. I wasn't going to look a gift cupcake in the mouth, so to speak. I smiled, nodded, and decorated.

After sampling all the desserts, Lily and I went upstairs, wrote up a couple of notes, got into our pj's, and talked for a bit. We were really pleased with the interviews. We thought that on Monday we could get a good start on the next chapter. We were both drowsy, so we put on a movie and fell asleep pretty early.

10/22 - somewhat-surly Saturday

It was a perfect day for the fall fundraiser. Lily and I planned to meet Amy, Imani, and Sara at eleven and hang out until about one, when I had to leave to get ready for soccer. Lily and I walked over to the high school. The colors that were still on the trees were gorgeous. Some had dropped leaves, creating little yellow, orange, or red carpets on the grass that Lily and I swished through. It was a perfect walk to the high school.

Amy, Imani, and Sara were waiting for us by the school entrance. We walked over to the pumpkins and picked out some cute little ones to buy and bring home. Then we went over to check out Audrey's stand. She had a big sign advertising "Gluten-Free and Glutinous Treats." Her table was doing a good business, crowded with buyers. We hung around, waiting our turn and chatting. After a while, Lily whispered, "Look behind you." I turned and saw Alexis, Taylor, and Lindsay.

Taylor said, "Hi guys!" like we had just hung out the day before. I smiled and turned back to talk to my group.

Alexis also said, "Hi."

But they got really quiet and awkward until Lindsay said, "You know, we've been talking and realized that we were kind of rude to you, Gaby, and to Lily too."

"You think?" I said. I wasn't in the mood to play nice.

Lily nudged me and said, "You know, it happens. Let's move on."

I was furious, but I didn't say a word, and moved up with my *real* friends to get some gluten-free and glutinous treats. We left Alexis, Taylor, and Lindsay and continued to walk around the fair. I was quiet and chomped on my magic bar while Lily talked away with AIS.

It was getting close to one o'clock, so I said a hasty good-bye and headed home.

I walked in a huff. I was really angry. How could Lily be so nice to those girls after they had been so mean to me, *and* to her? I started to kick leaves around, throwing a mini tantrum in my head. By the time I got home, I had just a few minutes to grab something to eat before soccer, and then I drove off with Dad to the game.

I was really quiet in the car. Dad used the opportunity to put some music on the radio that I hated, but I didn't feel like saying a word.

Soccer was a good opportunity to let off a bunch of steam, and I did it in a big way. I scored two goals and almost knocked over the midfielder on the other team.

On the ride home, Dad congratulated me on a good game. I just grumbled. "So what's up with you today?" he asked. "That moodiness really worked on the field, but it's time to let it go."

I glowered at him and through clenched teeth said, "I'm not moody." He was quiet for a long time and looked a little sad the way Dad gets when we snap at him. (I sometimes think that he's milking the sadness for sympathy points. And it works.)

"Well, I might be a *little* moody. Lily was really forgiving to some girls who have been kind of mean to both of us lately. We saw them at the fundraiser today, and the girls apologized for being snotty, and Lily said, 'Let's move on,' and I'm not sure that I want to move on."

"You know, Gaby," Dad said after a few minutes of silence, "everyone tries to do the best they can in their best moments. It's a lot easier to let things go than to hold on to bad feelings. It's easier said than done, but there are so many things to be bothered by. Isn't it better to have one off of your list?"

Now I was sorry that I'd even brought the whole thing up. I wasn't getting any sympathy from Dad on this one. But I did think about what he said for the rest of the day.

10/24 - miffed Monday

I was still annoyed with Lily. I had sulked during lunch and was still sulking in language arts. Ignoring me, Lily started to type:

CHAPTER FIVE: Contending

Lily looked at me and asked, "Do we do this chapter, or do we do the one about telling your friend that something's wrong with her?"

I became a little more subdued. "I just wish that you weren't so nice and so forgiving of Alexis, Lindsay, and Taylor, and that you didn't speak for me, because I haven't forgiven Lindsay or Taylor for dumping me at the beginning of the year!"

"Well, if you felt that way, you had plenty of chance to say something then and there, and now you're taking it out on me instead of them!" Lily said. "I don't feel like having enemies. I have no plans to be great friends with them, and I certainly don't trust them, but as long as they leave me alone, I can tolerate them. And you don't have to do what I do, and I don't have to do what you do…Isn't that the whole clique avoidance idea? We're friends and we're going to stick together no matter what. In the meantime, I can be just friendly enough to those girls, and you can do what you want. *Okay?*" She looked meaningfully at me.

"*All right!*" I said.

"You sure?" she said a little less assertively and a little more worried.

"Yeah. Let's 'move on,' as you say in your lingo." I smiled. Just as we were about to start the chapter, the bell rang.

"We better get a 'move on' this chapter tomorrow before we forget what we want to say," Lily said. "Come on, grouchy!" She smiled, and we changed classes.

10/26 - work-it Wednesday

We hadn't made any progress on the new chapter. We had all of these really good interview notes, but we just couldn't get started. We'd done a bunch of Internet searches, but nothing triggered our 'writing juices,' as Ms. Lamb likes to say.

We'd spent class time on the Internet, doing other homework, and when Ms. Lamb wasn't looking, playing the combination animal game. Finally, Lily said, "I've got it."

"Well—yay! Type it, please just type it!" I begged.

CHAPTER FIVE: Contending with Cliques

Do you recognize yourself or someone else as any of the below?

1. You're in charge. You don't let your friends have any friends that you don't approve of first.

Or

2. You do everything that your friend in charge (#1) tells you to do. You really want to be like them instead of yourself.

Or

3. You float between cliques. People like you, and you don't act bossy.

Or

4. You have your own opinions but you're afraid to do what you think is right if it goes against what #1–#3 do. You get caught in the middle when there is a fight in the clique.

Or

5. You'll do anything to get approval from the group, so you back them no matter what they do.

Or

6. You convince #1–#5 in the group that they can trust you and tell you their secrets, but you're not always trustworthy.

Or

7. You're the target of bullying by #1–#6. You could be in the clique or on the outside. Either way you wind up feeling alone.

We found these ideas credited to the book *Queenbees and Wannabees* by Rosalind Wiseman.

If you are any of the above or know of people like those above, then congratulations. You are experiencing "clique virus."

"Clique virus?" I started laughing.
"Let's lighten it up a bit and see where it takes us." Lily giggled. She was getting a little giddy. I took over.

We have discovered through intensive research and *interviews* (in italics for Ms. Lamb's benefit) that clique virus can show up anywhere.

It can crop up with people you thought were your closest friends. They look for someone they think is better than you, and in doing so, they forget how to be good friends.

It can crop up suddenly, when you find yourself in a group and all too soon, you don't have your own identities anymore.

It can crop up at the lunch table when someone new decides to join your group, and you and your friends don't even speak to him or her.

We added all of the stories that we heard during Audrey's baking spree, and then I typed:

It can mutate

"Mutate?" Lily asked.
"Shhh, I'm creating!"

It can mutate when two smaller groups glom onto each other, leave some others out, and create a *compound clique.*

"This is starting to sound like a sci-fi movie—*The Zombie Clique,*" Lily observed. I was having too much fun at this point to stop.

It knows no bounds. It affects kids and grown-ups alike. Just google "cliques in the workplace."

"The workplace really does seem to have a lot of the same problems that middle school has," commented Lily.

And our research tells us that it can also be found on the playground, and not only with kids, but with their moms or dads as well.

When I added the above, I said to Lily, "My mom told me a story about when she first had Audrey and took her to the playground with her. The women who were there were very, very picky about who they hung out with."

I remembered Aunt Mimi and the assisted-living gang, and typed:

> Clique virus can relapse long after you think you are done with it. Older people are not immune. We have heard that even in assisted-living homes, clique virus can be contagious.
>
> So…How do you combat clique virus? Here are some easy steps. They include advice from our panel of high school experts.
>
> If you find yourself in the middle of a clique:
>
> * Try to remember that these people are not the boss of you.
>
> * Keep up with friends who are outside of the clique, so that you still have the option to be with kids who treat you the way you want to be treated.
>
> * If you are the top dog in your group, think about setting the example for including others.

*   Don't let the clique talk you into giving up the things you like to do that don't involve the clique.

*   If you don't like what the clique is doing, speak up. If they don't like what you are saying, leave.

If you find yourself on the outside of a clique:

*   First of all, remember that whatever you do, don't panic. Being excluded could be the best thing that ever happened to you.

*   Don't take it personally. It has nothing to do with you and everything to do with the bad behavior of the clique.

*   Try to realize there could be many things going on in the clique that you are just not seeing. Be aware that some kids in the clique might feel badly about behaving exclusively. They may be afraid that if they don't follow along, the clique will gang up on them.

*   Realize that kids in cliques are not always having a lot of fun being bossed around by others.

* Instead of being on the outside and looking in, just walk away and find something that is actually fun to do.

* If you want to spend time with someone who is in a clique, invite them to do something with you. It is up to them to decide who they want to spend time with.

* Be a welcoming person to those around you, and you will find friends who want to be with you.

Lily added:

For more on this, go back to chapter one.

"Nice touch," I said, and then she added:

And remember…Don't take it personally.

11/2 - woeful Wednesday

I woke up yesterday with chills and a sore throat. Mom took one look at me and said, "Nope. No school today." I snuggled back down in bed, really glad to have a day to lie low. After a great sleepover at Lily's, we had a real fun Halloween night with LAISG *and* some boys from our grade who actually wanted to tag along with us (miraculous). I was pooped. Lucky for me I was sick enough to get a day off. Mom called it my *Halloween malaise*.

Today I was feeling better. Just as I was getting ready to leave for school, Lily texted me and said that she was skipping lunch today. She needed to finish studying for the social studies test, which, for her, was last period. I went from deep relaxation—or as deep as you can go on a school day—to instant panic. Not only did I completely forget about the test, I didn't even have a lunch period to get ready. My test was first period.

I skimmed through my options. Plead sick again—nope. Just told Mom how great I was feeling. Plead with the teacher for a make-up because I was sick yesterday—nope. That teacher has a heart of stone. Skip class and hide in a locker—nope. Locker's too small. Don't go to school and go visit Aunt Mimi—nope. Too far, and too many other problems. Tell Mom I forgot about the test—no way. There would be a huge lecture.

I told myself, "Face it. You're stuck!"

I raced out the door and blew past my crowd—wow, I actually have a crowd—and sat down in the library to furiously look over my notes in the ten minutes before the class started. I knew that the lowest grade in the semester could get thrown out. This would be it.

Ten minutes sometimes goes by really fast—actually, always, unless your sister is torturing you for some of your Halloween candy. The bell for first period rang, and I trudged to my social studies class. Mr. Rockowitz was already at his desk. He is a reasonably nice guy but has a no-excuses attitude for late homework and bailing out on tests.

"You all bright-eyed and bushy-tailed and ready to take this joy of a test?" he asked, smiling. I didn't even look up. He passed out the tests, and it all started. There were two essays and an alternative of filling in all of the states on the map.

Okay, I thought. *Gotta do the map because I have no idea what these essay questions mean, and we did go cross-country last summer, and I was awake for most of the ride, and...*

I realized that Mr. Rockowitz was looking at me because I had stopped looking at the test and was staring out the window. I quickly looked down and frantically started filling in states. *Alabama, North Daokta, New Hampshire*—no, that's on the end, and that other one is spelled wrong. *North Dakota. New York, Massachusetts, Denver...* no, *Colorado*. I was sweating. When every state was finally filled in, I saw that the next part of the test had even more definitions. Geography, equator, latitude, longitude, irrigation, climate...and the list went on. I was halfway through the list when the bell rang. I dropped off the test, not even looking at Mr. Rockowitz, and left for a relieving double period of math. Anything would be better than what had just happened in social studies.

At lunch I hung out with AIS and, as usual now, Kyle and Jon and Ted. I tried to forget that social studies existed. The rest of the day was a blur. Finally the day ended, and Lily and I walked home together after saying good-bye to AIS.

"That test was so easy," Lily said. I was really quiet. "Okay, let's start again," she said. "What did you think of the social studies test?

I sighed. "I completely forgot about it and remembered when you texted me this morning. Of course, *my* test was first period."

Lily gave me a hug. "Don't worry, Gaby. You know he drops the lowest grade, and there are always extra-credit somethings."

"Yeah. I guess. Talk later, okay?"

We went our separate ways. Now, on top of all my other school work and this dumb book project, I had to think about even more extra credit...ugh! I just wanted to get home to Scout, get a snack, and escape into a reread of *Harry Potter and the Chamber of Secrets* before starting on the pounds of homework.

Mom and Audrey were both home early and hanging around the kitchen table. *Great*, I thought. *Just when I was hoping for a day when my mom was still upstairs working and Audrey was off with whomever doing whatever, they're both here!*

I grabbed a snack and my book and tried to ignore them both. Actually, it turned out that they were both ignoring me. They were having a heated discussion. I was happy that they were leaving me alone and surprised that they already found the time to argue about something. Audrey couldn't have been home for more than ten minutes before me.

"You know, I really don't believe this," Audrey complained. "I do great in school, I'm home working diligently every school night, and just this one time, I want to go to Jake's house Friday night for a party, and I'm honest enough to tell you that his parents won't be home, but his older brother will be there. And what do you do? You take advantage of my honesty and say that if there's no parent there, I can't go!"

Mom leaned back from the table and looked at her thoughtfully. After a pause, she said, "Yes, that's what I'm telling you, and there should be no surprise there."

Audrey became red in the face. "You know, I might as well not try to work so hard. Where does it get me? The one time I try to ask for something, you can't be reasonable at all."

"Working hard is your decision, not mine," my mom batted back in response.

Really? I thought. *Then why am I told to work hard all of the time? These rules aren't fair.* I glanced back and forth at the two of them.

There was a long silence. Audrey was gearing up for a strong return. I saw her mind at work. "Well, thanks a lot!" she said. She pushed away from the table and went upstairs.

I was stunned. No volley. No line drive. No goal-scoring attempt. I was suspicious. I looked at Mom and she was just "moving on," to use Lily's favorite expression. She assumed that the game was over, and she had won. I wasn't so sure but was happy to be ignored until she turned to me. "So how was your day?"

Visions of wrong map answers danced in my head. "Oh fine," I said in as low-key a way as possible. "I had a social studies test this morning."

"I don't remember hearing about this test." She stared at me.

"Well, yeah, I kind of forgot about it."

"I knew all of that partying over the weekend and Halloweening on Monday would wipe you out," she replied quietly.

Not wanting to catch the tail end of her frustration with Audrey, I made motions to pack up and go hide in my room.

"Well-I've-got-a-lot-of-homework-see-you-later," I said quickly. Mom sighed and didn't say another word.

If I said that dinner was a happy-go-lucky experience, I would be so lying. Audrey had to be summoned out of her room. I had to share my test mishap once again with Dad. Mom tried to lighten the mood by running down to the basement to get more plastic wrap and being chipper about how she loved having extra grocery supplies on hand. (Supply-loving must be genetic.) She said that she felt like she was a pioneer on the prairie.

Audrey snapped back with, "Oh yes, the pioneers were always getting their plastic wrap from the pantry on the prairie."

Dad scowled at Audrey and then scowled at me. He told us that he and Mom were excusing themselves, and Audrey and I could deal with cleanup.

"But I have a lot of homework!" I said.

"Me too," Audrey whined in.

"Well, both of you have either forgotten about your assignments or have decided not to care as much. It would seem that you have plenty of time to clean up and do the dishes." With that, they left the room.

"Pains in the butt," Audrey muttered.

"Shh," I said. "Any more from us, and they might make us renovate the basement!"

She smiled at me. "We could build a panic room and put them in there every time they panic over something stupid."

I smiled back. "Well, at least now it's quiet down here."

"So what happened on the social studies test?" she asked.

"Oh, it was a disaster. I put Alabama next to Ohio and did many other unspeakable things." I rolled my eyes, and she laughed.

"Rock"—as she called my teacher— "is good for lots of extra credit. Don't worry."

"Just what I want…more work!" I said.

With the dishes finished, we went upstairs into our individual "chambers of homework horrors."

11/4 - fraught Friday

A truce has taken effect on the battlefield. No one at home is really being friendly, but the matter of Jake's party had died. Someone else's parent called Jake's mom to ask if there would be adult supervision, tipping off Jake's mom. Jake and his brother are grounded. Mom looked relieved when she heard this from Audrey. This sent Audrey storming back upstairs to her room last night.

I sat quietly at the dinner table, waiting for the inevitable "Did your test come back?"

"Yes. I flunked it, but Mr. Rockowitz joked to me when he handed it back: 'Well, it's clear that you didn't cheat on this test. Jon, who sits next to you, scored the highest grade, and you the lowest!'"

"Super," said a somewhat sarcastic Mom.

This morning found a silent bunch around the breakfast table. Eventually Mom said to me, "It's time for a quiet weekend at home to catch up on your work. After your last soccer game, I want you home this weekend." I didn't really have the heart to argue, because I was so loaded up with stuff to do that I needed the time anyway. Geez, this is only seventh grade. What on earth do these teachers have planned for us next year?

I left for school and met Lily on the way in. "Time for the next chapter. Do you want to work on it over the weekend?" she asked.

"Yeah, let's start in class today, and then why don't you come over on Sunday. I'm going to get a lot of school stuff out of the way on Saturday. I don't even know what chapter we should attempt next: 'My parents are making me miserable' or 'My school work is making me miserable.' Both are so relevant right now."

"We'll figure it out in class," she said.

We figured it out at lunch. We got onto the topic of the things that annoy us most and parents came up, so Lily and I decided to poll our panel of "experts."

"Okay, guys," Lily said, very businesslike. "What do your parents do that bugs you the most?" AIS, Kyle, Ted, and Jon all started talking at once.

"Okay, one at time," Lily said.

"Why so curious?" asked Jon.

"It's for the book project. Don't worry. Anything you say will be anonymous. It won't be held against you," Lily said, trying to make a joke. She paused, blushed, turned away from Jon, and asked Sara, "So, what were you saying?"

Hmm, I thought, *that chapter on boyfriends and girlfriends may need to come soon for Lily.*

Sara started. "My mom never stops asking me questions about everything I do. It drives me nuts!" The others followed with different complaints. By the end of lunch, we had our list for the next chapter, just in time for language arts class.

CHAPTER SIX: Problems with Parents

Into everyone's life some parent or guardian
annoyance must fall.

"Huh?" I was looking over Lily's shoulder as she started the next
chapter.

"Well, we want to be inclusive. Not everyone has parents,
but everyone has someone watching out for them," she said. I
grabbed the laptop.

A parent's job is to watch out for you, but when
the watching is too much, here are some tips to
deal with the situation. *Note that we are only
dealing with everyday problems of managing
your parents.

We remembered hearing about a kid in school who had been
having some serious problems with her parent treating her very
badly. I didn't think we were capable of handling that topic, but I
figured that we should include this next piece of advice.

There are sometimes more serious situations
where you may need to reach out to a trusted
teacher or guidance counselor.

So on to the everyday suggestions for navigating
your parents and their personality problems.

There are different parent personalities. Our seventh grade panel of "experts" shared their insights on the most common and annoying parent behaviors. Some of the parent personalities include all of the below traits at the same time. If that is the case, we are truly sorry for you. Read on and learn how to cope with:

The Question Asker, the Rule Imposer, and the Overinvolver

The Question Asker

Do you ever come home from school and want to settle down to a relaxing snack, and all of a sudden, your peace is interrupted by a phone call or an in-person interrogation session by your parent? It goes like this:

Who did you have lunch with?

What was your day like?

Where did you go during recess?

Why haven't you been spending time with (fill in the blank)?

When is that project due?

The first thing to remember is that these *are* annoying questions, and it is not just your imagination. So here are some thoughts on how to respond and finish up with the curious parent as soon as possible so you can get on with some relaxation.

Who did you have lunch with?

Two options exist here. You can tell them, if you are in the mood. Or you can say that you read at lunch and ask them who they had lunch with. This will very much surprise them and either put them on the defensive, or they will go off on their own story, which might be more interesting than yours.

What was your day like?

Many options here:

1. Your day was fantastic, and you want to tell them every highlight.

2. Your day was lousy, and you want to tell them every lowlight.

3. Your day was lousy, and you don't want to tell them anything. This is another situation where you tell them it was fine and immediately ask them how their day was. Their day may also

have been lousy, and they will then change the subject, leave the room, or end the phone call. Or their day may have been great, and you can listen to them instead of thinking about your day.

4. Take a chance and tell them that you just don't feel like talking right now. They understand being frazzled and will usually give you space.

Where did you go during recess?

Now this is a very loaded question. It could elicit a sarcastic response from you, resulting in a parent feeling sad and left out. So don't tell them you went fishing or to the mall, unless your parent appreciates sarcasm. Just smile and say, "I went to the library."

Why haven't you been spending time with (fill in the blank)?

Again, a complicated question. The soup that you just microwaved is getting cold, or your ice cream is melting. You just want to relax, and you have a parent who again seems very needy at this point in time.

1. You say that "Blank" is wanted in four states for identity theft. The parent will not be convinced or amused.

2. You say that you are not cool enough for "Blank" anymore. Regardless of whether this is true or false, you will get a lot of sympathy points.

3. You say that you are too cool for "Blank." We recommend against this. 'Blank" will get a lot of sympathy points, and you will get a lecture.

4. You shrug and stuff your snack in your mouth so you can't talk. You hope that your parent gets distracted and has to get back to whatever they were doing.

When is that project due?

This is a real fun parental question. It has two answers: "not for a while" and "I've got it covered." You then stuff your snack in your mouth because now they really know everything that they need to know.

The bell rang, and I looked up from typing. Lily was smiling. She said, "Someone has been tangling with their parents. Looks like this *is* the topic to do right now. We can finish this one up at your house on Sunday."

11/6 - super Sunday

Lily came over at eleven o'clock on the nose. I was feeling pretty good about my work-a-thon on Saturday. After soccer and an end-of-season pizza, I came home and charged through a bunch of homework. For social studies extra credit, I created a master map with all of the states (now with Alabama far away from Ohio) and their capitals. I started writing little paragraphs about each capital city. I had twenty done, and I'd finish up the rest by next week when the extra credit was due.

Lily and I went upstairs and continued to fill in suggestions for the other parental types that we'd identified.

The Rule Imposer

Do your parents make too many rules? Do the rules change daily, like dinner specials in a restaurant? If so, you have our sympathy. We do know that many rules are important, but *too* many are just *too* many.

It is hard to know what to do with the "Rule Imposer." After all, they are your parents, and they unfortunately are in charge. Here are a few strategies:

Try to reason with them. Sometimes in a weak parental moment, they may come around on one of their rules. If they do, give them a big hug. If you are particularly suspicious of their change of heart, try to get it in writing.

Be sensitive to the parental atmosphere.

"What on earth is that?" asked Lily.

"Ah! You don't have an older sister. I've had years of watching Audrey in action," I said and continued typing.

Don't try to change a rule with a particularly grouchy parent. It will backfire.

Try to tell your parent what rules some of your friends have but only pick the friends your parents really like. Regardless, they may say what any parent under siege would say, namely, "I don't worry about what other kids can do."

Try to find another parent who your parent really likes or admires and say, "But your really good friend, 'other mom,' does this." This may stir up some parental competition, and your parent may be more easily persuaded.

If all else fails, gently guide them to a few relevant websites. Approach the parent cautiously. Smile and hand them a list. It can include the following:

16 Signs that You Are Too Strict with Your Kids

Are You a Tiger Mom?

Negative Effects of Too Many Rules on Children

"Which ones did Audrey do?" asked Lily.
"All of the above," I replied.
"Which ones worked?"
"Not sure," I admitted.
Lily then typed:

And—good luck.

The Overinvolver

There exists a species of parent who for whatever reason really wants to relive their middle school experience. When you come home from school and they return from work, they eagerly shuffle through your backpack and study your assignments. They long for a return to that challenging word problem that they can now ace. They bring their very own set of markers, glue, and poster board downstairs at project time. If you sense this behavior in your parent, here are some suggestions.

I looked over her shoulder. "Aren't you going a little overboard?"

"Well, we do want to make the book interesting." Lily continued typing.

Suggestion #1- If they are so excited to help, just walk away and turn on the TV or go read a book. You can say, "I see that you've got this covered."

Suggestion #2- Tell them kindly that you think that they may be avoiding their own chores. There must be something else that they could be doing right now.

I started laughing and took over the typing:

Suggestion #3- Say, "Okay, fine. You seem to want a lot of involvement in my life. So you can be very involved in my project/schoolwork/ etc., and I will go out with you on date night and hang out at your next book club meeting when you talk about that racy novel that you are reading."

Lily giggled. We went on to fill in additional suggestions for the other parent behavior groups. At the end of the chapter, we added something I remembered from a "conversationargument" that Audrey once had with my mom. Audrey had told Mom, "It isn't my job to make your anxiety go away." So I wrote:

> Remember that parents do all of the above to relieve their own worries about us. However, they occasionally can care just a little bit too much. Tell them in as kind a way as possible that you can't always make them feel better about the things that that worry them. Sometimes they just have to trust that we know what we're doing.

Lily read it and liked it. After finishing "Problems with parents," we hung out for the rest of the afternoon.

11/15 - tuning-up Tuesday

We had a week off from chapter writing. Ms. Lamb was out sick at the beginning of last week, and we had some standardized test stuff. An added plus of standardized testing was that there was *noooooo* homework. Lily and I hung out a lot after school, sometimes with Wonder at her house, sometimes with Sara, Imani, and Amy at one of their houses, and sometimes at my house. It was a great week.

On Sunday after breakfast, Mom started talking about our favorite family holiday of the year, Thanksgiving. She pulled out this overstuffed folder of recipes and started thumbing through while she was sharing preparation strategy. "Okay, team. So, this year both grandmas and grandpas are coming, Uncle Craig and his family"—Dad's brother, who was lots of fun to be around—"Aunt Mimi, and she wants to bring her new friend Olga, and of course, Jack."

"Oooh! Mimi has a boyfriend!" Audrey said.

"So that makes fourteen," Mom continued. "Not too bad.

"We have ten days before the holiday starts. No one is sleeping over this year, because everyone has things to do on Friday, so we'll aim to start around noon with…" She looked up. No one was listening anymore. We had grabbed the recipes and were starting to pull out all of our favorites. Dad had gone back to reading the paper. Mom smiled. "Okay, girls, why don't you make up the menu, and we can all look it over and then make a shopping list."

Audrey and I were happy to have this job. It was really fun because in addition to picking our favorites, we could look back on a few of the recipe "misses" that we had tried before and would never try again. We also could experiment and throw in one or two new ideas.

"Do you remember making pumpkin soup last year?" Audrey asked.

"What was wrong with that?" I asked.

"Well, it tasted pretty good, but we were blending pumpkin for hours!"

Mom sighed. "I remember the first Thanksgiving that Dad and I put together right after we were married. I was convinced that stuffing required egg yolks and wound up putting in about ten of them and baking it before I finally read that the recipe called for none."

Dad smiled and said, "It still tasted okay."

"You just don't remember." Mom smiled back at him.

"What about Audrey's cranberry sauce?" I teased.

"Yeah—and what was the problem with that?" she asked.

"Well," I said, "it's my favorite side, but it always boils over, and all of the cooking spoons are now stained red."

"The most important word in that sentence is *favorite*," Audrey replied dryly.

Mom started giggling uncontrollably. We all looked over at her. "Michael, do you remember the year that you singed your eyebrows basting the turkey?" We looked at Dad. He does have rather bushy eyebrows, so this was pretty easy to imagine.

"Yup, but not so funny at the time." Dad grinned.

"And Mom…" Audrey cleared her throat. "This year, let's just be a little more, how should I say this…Zen, like more relaxed, about the day of organizing. It's just a dinner, not a military offensive."

Mom blushed. "Okay, I do get a little worked up about the planning."

"A little!" Dad started to say, but Mom shot him such a look that he immediately stopped speaking.

Audrey continued, "It doesn't matter who sits where and which chair goes in which spot, and—"

"Okay, I get it. Zen you want, and Zen you'll get!" Mom said.

Audrey and I added the favorite roll recipe to the pile and started arguing about who would pound the dough and what time to wake up to get them started. Mom now cleared her throat. "Zen, remember."

After another twenty minutes of sorting and composing, we had our menu plan and the shopping list set up.

I am going to try to make a blueberry pie. You might ask why blueberry for Thanksgiving? Well, Dad really likes blueberry pie. We're adding that to our pumpkin and pecan pie production, which Dad hates, so as not to make him feel unrepresented. Audrey brought up the topic of "seasonally appropriate pie," but Dad looked at her, and she stopped talking. Let's just see how Zen this will really be!

Back in class today, Lily and I started to plan which chapter we would do next. As a stalling tactic, Lily suggested that we create our table of contents. Happy to procrastinate, I started to type:

105

Chapter One: Combatting Shyness

Chapter Two: Winning with Making Friends

Chapter Three: Beating the Bully and the "Cy-bore" (boring kids on the Internet with nothing better to do than) Bully

Chapter Four: Beating Yourself Up—Stop!

Chapter Five: Contending with Cliques

Chapter Six: Problems with Parents

"It all sounds so violent," Lily said.

"Well, middle school is serious business," I replied. "They send us poor defenseless kids as young as ten off into the cold, cruel world of middleschoolness."

"Middleschoolness." Lily smirked.

"Well, yeah. And who is telling any of them, any of us for that matter, how to manage all of these problems? No one! That's who!" I was getting dramatic.

Lily considered this. "True, true...Well, then, we have a real gem here."

"I wouldn't go that far," I said hastily. "But we do have a guide to dealing with 'midlife school' crisis."

"Okay, so what should the title be?" she asked.

I thought for a minute. "The title should be *The Best Middle School Self-Defense Book Ever.*"

Lily contemplated this and then said, "I like it. I love it."

I smiled. "Well, so much for procrastinating. Let's do the next chapter on teachers and school work."

CHAPTER SEVEN: The Trouble with Teachers

I looked up at Lily, and she looked back at me. How to proceed? I began typing.

> The great thing and not-so-great thing about middle school is that you no longer have only one teacher for all of your classes. It's great because you don't have to be stuck all year with one crabby teacher, if that was your situation. Now, with any luck, some of the day will be filled with some less-crabby teachers, and some really good ones.

"Remember," said Lily, "Ms. Lamb is going to read this."

"Okay," I said, and I added the next sentence.

> Of course one should always be so lucky to have some great teachers like Ms. Lamb, but this can't always happen.

"Well, hopefully that's worth a few brownie points," Lily said.

"Doubtful," I replied. We scoured the Internet to find all of the different types of difficult teachers that we could.

After looking on the Internet, we decided that our teachers weren't so bad and that there were some really awful teacher stories out in cyberspace. We came up with topics like:

The "I think I'm so much fun" teacher

The crabby teacher

The boring teacher

The teacher who thinks he/she is a rock star

The teacher who would rather be somewhere else

The bell rang. We didn't get much done. "Do you want to come over and work on this for a while at my house?" I asked.

"Yeah. Let me check with my mom after school," said Lily.

Lily's mom texted her back a yes and said that she would pick her up by six. I walked in the house with Lily. Audrey was just sitting down with a snack. She looked up and remarked, "Greetings, aliens."

Lily was getting used to Audrey's sense of humor and replied, "Greetings, Voldemort."

"So what are you two up to?" Audrey asked.

"Lily's going to hang here until six. We have another chapter of this book project due."

"Did you check with Mom to see if it's okay?" she asked.

"Oh. I'll call Mom." I then called Mom, who said she really couldn't talk, but it was fine.

I opened my laptop and the attachment with our latest chapter. Lily and I huddled over the screen, at a loss of where to go next. Audrey stood over our shoulders and read out loud. "The trouble with teachers…" She was quiet for a moment and then read more. "The crabby teacher, the boring teacher…"

She then walked around to the other side of the table, saying, "No, no, no, no, no!" She sat down. "Get a snack and let's have a chat."

We pulled out a bag of popcorn, filled a bowl, and waited for what seemed like a very long pause from Audrey. She took a deep breath. "You can't set this chapter up this way. You have a teacher, whom you need on your side, even if she isn't any of these types of teacher. She'll think that you're being too critical. You don't want to call out any teachers. You need to go at this in a different way."

I wanted to disagree with her, but the fact of the matter was that we had absolutely no idea what to do with the rest of the chapter. "So what should we do?" asked Lily through a full mouth of popcorn.

"First slide some of that over," said Audrey. The popcorn flew across the table. "I think you should make the topic about school work stress. That way you aren't attacking, but getting sympathy points."

Lily and I chewed and mulled over what she said. Audrey sat back, folded her arms, and waited for us.

"She's so right," Lily said.

"Yeah, I think so too."

"My work here is done," Audrey said. "I'll be upstairs if you need anything. And hey, I want to read this masterpiece of yours when you guys finish." She left before I could say anything.

Lily deleted the first part of the chapter.

"Different plan," she said as she started typing. "Let's earn some sympathy points."

CHAPTER SEVEN: Dealing with School Stress

Along with all of the adjustments a middle schooler has to make regarding cliques and bullies and body image and changes in friends, there is the issue of why middle school exists in the first place, and that is to provide the enormous

She looked up, grinned at me, and continued:

amount of homework, pop quizzes, tests, projects, and classroom participation, which can be overwhelming and exhausting and never-ending. Between the social stress and the work stress, the pressure can be paralyzing.

She sat back, and I said, "Cool."

All of this, in addition to all of our extracurricular activities, can create a lot of anxiety for us.

"Excellent!" I added.

After a seven-hour school day and then sometimes another hour or two of extracurriculars, we come home to at least an hour or more of homework.

I looked something up, and then typed:

> The Bureau of Labor Statistics has a pie chart that says the average parent spends 8.8 hours a day working. If you add up kid work hours, which include seven hours of school and one hour (at least) of homework, without including extracurriculars, we already have them beat. This is why after a long day of work, when our parents are sitting back and reading the paper or watching television, we are still doing homework. Understandably, we are pooped, and stressed.

I stopped and looked at Lily. She smiled. "Sympathy points."

> So what do you do to cope with school-work stress?

"What *do* you do?" I asked Lily. I went back to the Internet. "Look here. There's an article written in 1998, and here's one from 1980. That's thirty years ago. They still haven't figured out what to do about all of this stress. Geez!" I searched some more sites.

"Not helping us," said Lily.

I kept searching. "Okay, I have a plan," I said. "We'll write about signs of stress. I just found a WebMD article on relieving stress."

"Fire away!" Lily said.

> First of all, you may have a lot of stress, but you don't realize it. If you have a lot of stomachaches or a lot of headaches, you could really be having a stress attack. If you overreact to a situation, it could be a sign of stress.

I remembered how I had lashed out at Mom about the Halloween carrots and realized that I really had been stressed about my friend issue back then. Life was feeling a lot better now.

> Trouble sleeping and frequent nightmares are also signs that school pressure could be getting to you. Trouble concentrating or focusing, and trouble completing school work and not wanting to go to school, are other indications of stress.

"Well, if not wanting to go to school and staying cozy in bed is an 'indication,' I must be stressed beyond belief!" I joked. Lily was now on a roll and ignored me.

> If you think that you are alone in feeling stressed out by school work, then you are wrong. Different articles on the Internet report varying levels of stress related to homework, ranging from 38 percent to a whopping 89 percent of kids reporting homework stress.

So since stress is here and it is here to stay, here
are some ways to cope.

Take a power nap. If you can get a twenty-minute nap in after school, it will help to recharge
you for getting your homework done.

"Look at this!" I was busy googling. "This school has a
'Power Nap Club.' Its motto is, 'I came, I saw, I slept.'" Lily
laughed, added it to her paragraph, and continued:

High school students in a Power Nap Club
report feeling relaxed after a twenty-minute nap
in a classroom where soft music is playing.

Stress management tips from About.com also
include the following:

1. Visualization, or thinking about anything but
school work

The second part was our addition.

To visualize, get into a really comfortable position.

Lie down or get into a comfy chair. Take deep
breaths that expand your belly, hold for a count
of six, and exhale. Repeat twice.

Once you feel comfortable, picture yourself in
the most relaxing place you can be. Examples

are floating on ocean waves or being in front of
a cozy fireplace.

"Sounds like a lot of work to do all of this relaxing," Lily
said.
"Shh. I'm concentrating!" I took over typing.

> Then try to involve all of your senses. What
> does the place look like; what does it smell and
> sound like?

> Stay in this place for as long as you like.
> When you are ready to "come back to earth,"
> count backward from twenty and tell your-
> self that when you get to "one," you will feel
> relaxed and alert and enjoy the rest of your
> day.

Lily was restless and fidgeting. I looked up at her, and she
stopped. I continued typing.

> Important tip: you might want to set an alarm
> so you don't fall asleep or "zone out" for longer
> than you planned.

"So…once you are nice and relaxed, this alarm blows you
back into reality?" Lily asked.
"This particular option may not be the one for you, Lily!" I
was getting a little annoyed with her.
"Okay, fine!" Lily snapped back. We were quiet. She started
typing.

2. Exercise

Exercising is a great way to destress. Walking, biking, yoga-ing, or even dancing around your room lets you unwind before sitting down with that wonderful homework project.

3. Breathing

In any situation where you feel stressed, breathing is a great way to relax. Try the breathing exercise that was mentioned before for a few minutes. It's a great way to unwind.

Lily typed away and was very quiet. I wasn't saying anything either. I think we were both a little testy.

"Music…" Lily said through clenched teeth. "And why don't you take over typing for a while!"

"Well, okay, I will!" I said, glaring at her.

4. Music

Listening to music is a great way to relieve stress.

I remembered that my sixth-grade math teacher would play classical music while we did math problems. I thought about mentioning this to Lily, but I wasn't in the mood to chat, so I typed away while Lily looked over my shoulder.

5. Progressive muscle relaxation (PMR)

When you are wound up or trying to relax before bedtime, PMR is a great way to unwind. Start by tensing all of the muscles in your face and then relaxing them slowly. Clench your teeth.

"Already clenched," Lily said, and looked at me. "Hey, let's take a break and try this. We both want to murder each other at this point. Let's see if PMR will help us relax. So it says that right before your test, clench your teeth and squeeze your eyes shut as tightly as possible, and grimace as hard as you can, and inhale for the count of eight. Then exhale and let your face completely relax. I'll go first."

She clenched everything in her face. I looked at her and started laughing.

"What's so funny?"

"Wait—let me show you. Do it again."

Lily clenched her face again, and I took a picture of her with my phone. She looked at the photo and also started laughing. "Imagine doing this in class right before a test. The teacher would send you to the nurse's office right away."

"Okay, Gaby, now you try it, and I'll snap you." I grimaced in between giggles, and Lily got the shot. We looked at our photos and both laughed.

"Okay, now let's try it together for real," she said. So we grimaced and inhaled, and counted to eight and exhaled. Then we tightened our neck muscles and inhaled, and counted to eight and exhaled. We giggled a lot, but it felt pretty good. We added the additional instructions:

> Continue with the rest of these groups of muscles: chest, belly, right arm and fist, left arm and fist, butt, and right leg and left leg.
>
> If you don't have time to tense all of these muscles because you will miss your test, just try the face and neck together, or shoulders and arms, or belly and chest, or butt, legs, and feet. If you start getting anxious that you are still running out of time before your test by doing all of this, you may consider saving this exercise for bedtime.

"Really!" said Lily. "It sounds like doing this will wipe you out and make you ready to sleep." She paused and then said, "Sorry I was snippy before."

"Yeah, me too," I said. "All this writing about stress is stressful!" She laughed, and then added a suggestion from Ask.com:

> 6. Stay organized
>
> Looking at a lot of clutter can be stressful. Try to keep your homework and study area clean and soothing and free of distractions. Many kids on websites say that starting on homework sooner rather than later is a good way to avoid becoming overwhelmed with too many projects at once.

I typed some ideas that my mom has suggested to me. Unfortunately, I rarely followed this advice.

> Create a neat pile of what to do, grab the first thing on the pile, do it, and move on to the next. Walk away from the pile for a break, and when you come back to it, you will be happy to see that it is smaller.

> Sometimes, if you get "blocked" on a project, walk away from it. You may need some time to let the plan for moving forward weave itself into your head.

"Put that project down and step away," Lily said in a stern police officer's voice. She then added a suggestion of her own:

> 7. Lighten up

> Find a good friend and have a good laugh. Laughing and joking around with a friend is a really great way to relax and relieve stress. Sometimes even doing homework with friends makes it a less stressful experience.

She looked up, and I said, "That's the best one of all!" We added one more line:

> If you aren't finding relief from your stress, talk to your parents or guidance counselor. They will help you figure out what to do next.

11/17 - trouble-thinking Thursday

Back in class, Ms. Lamb said she would give extra credit for chapters handed in early. Lily and I were feeling pretty good about our self-defense book, but we had one smallish problem: Ms. Lamb wants ten chapters in total, but along the way one of our chapters took up three topics. I call it "The Chapter That Ate the Planet." We have no idea what our last chapter is going to be.

Rather than worry about it now, we decided to move on with a chapter we'd planned about how to deal with friend fights. We had barely avoided a fight ourselves while doing the stress chapter. I started typing. Lily put her head down on folded arms and waited to see what would come out of me next.

CHAPTER EIGHT: Fixing Fights with Friends

"Go for it," she exclaimed. Ms. Lamb looked over at our table, and it was not a friendly glance. "Oops, sorry," Lily said and then whispered, "All right!" in my ear. As she did, she caught Jon's grin, and she blushed.

"I think someone has a crush on someone, and I'm not sure who," I said in my best Southern drawl.

Lily ignored me. "Come on, let's do fights."

"Okay." I decided not to tease her anymore just then. Extra credit was riding on fighting, so I started:

It's been a long week at school.

"As always!" I said while typing. Lily leaned in, probably happy not to be teased about Jon and eager to see what would happen next.

Lunch period is up next. You are looking forward to a nice, enjoyable lunch with your best friend, Blank. Another friend comes up to you and says, "Guess what BestBlank said?"

"*Blank* again?" asked Lily, but then said quickly, "Go on."

You say, "What?" She tells you she heard from someone else that BestBlank made fun of you. BestBlank said mean things about your clothes, hair, shoes; you name it. You march into the cafeteria, slam your books down, tell BestBlank that you are furious with her, and then you walk off in a huff. BestBlank had been having a very peaceful sandwich and has no idea what has just happened and also has no idea what to do.

"So what do they do?" Lily asked when I looked up from the keyboard.

"No clue," I said. "But it's attention-catching, right?"

"Yup," Lily said. "Time for some googling."

She spent a few minutes searching and then said, "Got it. I love you, wikiHow!" She took over typing, and now I was absorbed watching the screen.

> So now what? A few days go by, and neither one of you is speaking to the other. BestBlank is now mad as well, because how dare you act snooty and walk away like that. After another day or so, both you and BestBlank start to miss hanging with each other, but neither one of you wants to back down. Finally, you realize that you would rather spend time with BestBlank than be mad at her (or him).

"I love your gender neutrality," I said.

Lily typed on and said, "Well, both boys and girls fight, right?"

> Here are some steps to deal with the situation above, and other situations where you want to end a fight with a friend:
>
> * First, just be quiet for a while until you are less angry. This way you don't create another layer of fighting to get through. You can wind up saying so many bad things to each other that the real reason for the fight is buried under the new nasty stuff.

* Decide if that friend is really someone you want to spend time with. If you are always in a fight with them over something, then this fight might be the perfect chance for you to get rid of that friend.

"Make that a little clearer. It sounds like you want to lock them up in a dungeon," Lily said.

"Not a bad idea." I smiled and continued.

* Think about what you've done. Have you even bothered to tell your friend what the problem is? Have you done something to upset him or her? Do you even know if poor BestBlank said that stuff in the first place?

"Lots of questions, Gaby. I feel the drama," joked Lily.

"I feel the extra credit," I said.

Lily must have felt the extra credit too, because she took over and started typing furiously.

* Tell your friend that you're sorry for the mis-understanding and then say, "Let's make up and figure this out." BestBlank either will be happy to make up, which means that they still want to be your friend, or not interested. If they are happy then you can start to move forward. If they aren't happy, then maybe BestBlank is really not BestBlank, and it is time for a new best friend.

*   Try not to yell when you talk to your friend. Try to talk calmly about the problem without a cheering section around. Some kids love to watch a good fight, and that doesn't help the situation.

*   Don't try to make your friend jealous while you are in the process of fixing your fight. That doesn't really do anything but make the fight last longer.

*   Finally, know this: most fights are usually about something silly. So just make up, if that's what you want to do. Understand what went wrong and move on.

*   Here are some more tips for avoiding unnec- essary fights with friends. These come from the PBSkids help website. They give advice to kids and teens.

She looked up for my reaction. "Sounds important," I said. She nodded and continued:

*   Understand that your friend's opinions are as important as your own.

*   Deal with the fact that your friend has their own personality and most of the time that is what makes you really like them.

*   Let your friend have their own way once in a while.

*   Be understanding if your friend wants to do something with someone else instead of you sometimes. You don't want to get sick of each other.

*   Be loyal to your friend. Make sure that they know that they can count on you.

*   Let your friend know if you need some space, so they don't think that you are avoiding them. Tell them that you are busy today and tomorrow, and it is okay to do other things for a bit, but you will do something together very soon.

*   Never tell other kids a secret that your friend tells you.

Extra credit, here we come.

"Delete that, Lily."
"Oh, okay!"

11/18 - again finally Friday!

What is better than getting EC for turning in a chapter early? Getting EC and having it be Friday—except…

Lily and I sat in class again and mulled over what we wanted the next chapter to look like. We were really unsure of how to take on the 'Boys don't like me; girls don't like me' chapter. Watching Lily and Jon smile a lot at each other made me think that there might be one less girl and one less boy included in the chapter. The chapter also needed a better title.

"I don't know. I just don't know!" Lily said. "I don't know what to call this chapter. I don't know what we should put in this chapter. So what are you doing this weekend?"

"Well, both sets of my grandparents are back in town for Thanksgiving week, so I think we're going to see them tomorrow. On Sunday, we'll probably do some shopping for the holiday. How about you?"

"My aunt, her partner Chris, and my little cousin Gina are coming to stay with us for the week," Lily said.

"What do you mean by 'partner'?" I asked.

"Oh, they're gay," said Lily.

"Oh," I said. I was glad that Lily answered me before I asked if they worked in a law firm or something.

Lily was going on about how cute her little cousin was and how excited Emily was about seeing her. "…and I guess that means we can't get together to work on the book this weekend."

"Yeah, but let's figure out what to do with this next chapter on boyfriend and girlfriend stuff," I said. "If you have any ideas, text me."

Lily said sure, but sounded kind of pessimistic. I knew how she felt. I had no ideas at all.

When I arrived home from school, my mom was already there and said that tomorrow we would do one of our marathon grandparent days. First, my mom's parents at lunch, and then on to my dad's parents for dinner. I was excited because I hadn't seen them in a long time. I was looking forward to the great desserts that Grandma Ella, my mom's mom, always baked. I was also looking forward to dinner and the candy cabinet at Grandma Rose's house. (My mom looks forward to this probably more than I do.)

11/19—so-much-eating Saturday

On Saturday morning we were out by eleven to start the day that Dad called "The Grandparent Olympic Dining Tryouts." Audrey and I sat in the backseat and zoned out for the forty-five-minute ride to Grandma Ella and Grandpa Mick's house. I was mulling over how to tackle the next chapter and asked my mom and dad to retell the story of how they met. They had been a guy and a girl once, even though they're my parents.

Mom got all mushy and said that one of her best friends from college sat them together at her wedding. "Dad knew right away that he wanted to go out with me, and the first good thing about him was that he actually called when he said he would."

"*That's so good?*" I interrupted.

"You'd be surprised," Mom said. "Then he became a lot more serious about dating than I was, and it took me a little time to catch up." She smiled and looked over at Dad.

"How could she not immediately know that I was the best thing for her?" Dad asked. Mom leaned over and kissed him on the cheek.

"Okay, guys! No more lovefest," Audrey said. There were more smiles from the front seat, and the backseat went back to zoning out.

Before we knew it, we arrived. After a lot of hugs, a huge lunch with many courses and fantastic desserts, Grandpa showing off his new iPad, and my giving him a tutorial on what exactly to do with apps, we bundled up and dragged our full bellies into the car for the one-hour ride to Grandma Rose and Grandpa Harry's.

"Eating Olympics part two," Dad said. "And just in time to get our stomachs nice and stretched out for Thanksgiving."

Out of the car and into another cozy home. This one had more hugs, great food, three full candy dishes, and two different souvenir T-shirts with maps of Canada and Florida from various trips in their Winnebago. There were comments from my dad on how great the Winnebago sounded, and more comments from Mom, including, "Never in a million years!"

Then we were back in the car driving home. Audrey and I were in a food stupor. I was dozing until Audrey nudged me and asked, "Why are you asking everyone how they met? Is it for your opus?"

"Huh?" I asked.

"You know, the book!" Audrey said impatiently.

"I dunno. I guess," I said.

Grandpa Mick had told me he liked the way Grandma E walked. He was introduced to her through his sisters.

"Yes!" Grandma had said. "And your sisters told me to stay away from you, because you weren't—how do you say it these days— 'boyfriend material.'"

Grandma Rose had mentioned that she had met Grandpa H at a party. "He was a great dancer," she'd added.

Audrey smiled. "Those were great war stories about crushes."

"That's it!" I exclaimed, startling everyone out of their food fog. "That-is-it!" I grabbed Audrey and hugged her, and then I texted Lily. "Got it! Tty when I get home."

Later that evening, I was sprawled on my bed with my phone, rubbing my stomach and very pleased with myself. "So here it is, Lily. Listen to this," I said. "We don't know anything about boyfriend and girlfriend things, but we can write stories about how different people we know met. And Audrey mentioned something that gave me a great idea for the title of the chapter!" I paused for effect. "Chapter Nine: War Stories from the Crushes' Front Lines."

There was silence on the other end of the line, and then Lily said, "Perfect! It goes so well with our battle theme. We can ask everyone for stories at Thanksgiving and include them in the chapter. All of our searching on this topic has pretty much told us that no one has any good advice on getting boyfriends and girlfriends."

She continued. "They all say 'it just happens,' whatever 'it' is. And everyone says that everyone is awkward at some point. I just love this idea."

"Great," I said. "We can start it on Monday and then finish it on Saturday or Sunday of Thanksgiving weekend. That way, all of this stuff will be fresh in our minds. Plus, we have to finish these last two chapters in two weeks. Wouldn't it be great to get some EC by handing them in early?"

"It would be great to get this project out of the way and actually get together to have some fun for a change," Lily said.

I know how she felt. I was very ready to finish this thing up as well.

So we knew what we wanted to do—get stories about crushes—and we knew how we were going to do it, by getting all of the stories we could over Thanksgiving. What we didn't know how to do was start this chapter. We looked online for a while and finally just ended up staring at each other, because by this time we had explored every inch of each other's bags, had drawn every animal combination possible, and couldn't think of any other stalling activity.

I took in a deep breath and said, "Let's just be real."

"What does *real* mean?" Lily asked. I started typing:

CHAPTER NINE: War Stories from the Crushes' Front Lines

"Chapter nine! So exciting!" she said.

"Not as exciting as the end of Chapter ten will be," I said.

What on earth do two seventh graders know about giving crush advice?

Lily was about to interject but then seemed to realize that she had nothing to say.

Well, what does anyone really know about giving crush advice? Google gives 576,000,000 entries for the question, "How do you tell someone you like them?" We saw that everyone—old or young, girl or boy—has been on the Internet asking for that advice.

In addition, if you like someone and don't know how to get them to like you, you have a lot of company. The search "How do I get someone to like me?" turned up 2,120,000,000 results.

We decided that the best way to get information was to ask couples who are on the front lines and get firsthand accounts of how they met and hear what advice they have to share.

I looked up. Lily grinned. "Well, Ms. Lamb said to write what you know. In this case, we'll write what everyone else knows. We'll meet after Thanksgiving."

11/27 - more-stuffing Sunday

Day three of great leftover meals. I woke up and made myself a cranberry sauce, turkey, and stuffing sandwich on one of the awesome rolls that we baked for Thanksgiving. Mom looked at my towering sandwich. "I can't believe that you guys want to eat this stuff for breakfast!" Audrey and Dad were busy making their own leftover creations and reminiscing about Thanksgiving highlights. Uncle Craig and his family wound up staying over until last night. This was our first chance for a Thanksgiving recap.

"My favorite part of the day was watching Aunt Mimi and Jack flirting with each other, and watching great football," Dad said. "And the meal of course!" he added hastily.

Mom said, "My favorite part of the day was afterward during cleanup when you three and Mimi were watching football. Jack was with the rest of us cleaning up in the kitchen. We kept hearing, 'How did he not catch it? How did he not catch it? Unbelievable!'"

Mom continued: "Jack said, 'How did he not catch it? If any *us* were there, I'm sure we would have been able to do it. I'm sure that my darling Mimi would be up for the Most Valuable Player award or whatever these guys get!'"

We all laughed. "Jack is adorable." Audrey said. "Aunt Mimi picks good boyfriends!"

We were all in the kitchen munching as I gathered together my crush notes and waited for Lily to come over. Thanksgiving was lots of fun, and the weekend had gone by quickly from one leftover meal to the next.

Lily came in just as I was savoring the last few bites of my sandwich creation. She said, "I never, ever want to see cranberry sauce again!" She then proceeded to tell us about her little sister Emily, or "the tornado" as she calls her, and her adventures in the kitchen.

"So, on Friday we're all sitting around the table and Emily is dashing from one part of the kitchen to the other, putting out napkins, chattering with everyone, talking about her dance class, and showing off for my cousin Gina. My aunts were out shopping, my dad was also running errands, and my mom was telling Emily to slow down. Emily was busy bringing every left-over to the table. There were eight dishes at the table, and just the four of us at home. Mom had told Emily for the nth time to slow down when Emily, still talking about her dance class, takes this big bowl of cranberry sauce out of the refrigerator, pulls the plastic off, and then says, 'Look at this great move.' Mom is bringing over some plates, and I'm bringing drinks. Suddenly Emily does this wild spin, and the cranberry sauce flies out of the bowl, bounces off a wall, and splatters all over the kitchen. And I mean everywhere: the walls, the floor, a chair. If it was within three feet of Emily, it was hit!" Lily paused.

I was covering my gaping mouth, my mom had an expression of great sympathy, probably for Lily's mom, and my dad and Audrey were trying not to laugh.

Lily continued her story: "There was dead silence for about five seconds. It felt like forever. My mom walked out of the house and into the yard. We all ran after her to see what she was doing. She was walking in circles and counting to ten. She then headed back toward the house. We all ran back to the kitchen and watched my mom come in. Emily started to apologize. My mom listened to her and then said, 'Okay, guys, let's clean this up.'"

Lily turned to me. "Do you know how cranberry sauce turns everything red?" Audrey shot me a warning glance, and Lily continued, "We might never have cranberry sauce in our house again!

"But I did get some good stories for our chapter," she added.

"I can't wait to read this thing," Audrey said.

Lily looked very pleased with the opportunity to show off our work. "We'll send it to you when we're done."

I wasn't sure that I wanted Audrey to see it, but I was more focused on hearing Lily's stories and sharing mine. "Okay, let's go upstairs and get started," I suggested.

Once upstairs, Lily and I sat on my bed and exchanged a bunch of stories. I continued typing the chapter:

We had the opportunity to interview many couples.

We were "thankful" that there were so many people at our homes at Thanksgiving to interview.

Perhaps it won't surprise you that none of the couples met in the following ways:

1. At a ball after being magically dressed by a fairy godmother.

2. After being forced to live in a house with a hairy beast, which was then tamed.

3. After being poisoned, being dead, and then being kissed.

4. After kissing someone who's been asleep for one thousand years.

5. After seeing the girl of your dreams, finding a genie to help you because you aren't good enough to get her on your own, and flying on a magic carpet.

6. After living under the sea and finally living on earth and stalking someone until they meet you; and being able to live with them happily ever after.

"Any more Disney movies you want to add?" Lily asked. "Nope," I said and continued.

Below are some ways that our couples *did* meet. We grouped our couples into two categories as follows:

Group One - Situations that won't happen until years from now.

Lily dictated some of the stories from her Thanksgiving interviews:

> We met at work.

> We met in college when the two people we were dating broke up with us to date each other, and we started dating. They eventually broke up, but we stayed together.

I added Aunt Mimi's story:

> We met when I moved into my new apartment at the assisted living facility.

"We won't be in that situation for years and years," Lily said. She continued dictating:

> We met at a party. My friends really liked him and told me that I had to go out with him.

> We were friends in college. I liked him, and I told him so.

"Another college story. I'm impressed that she just told him that she liked him. How direct is that?" Lily said.

> We met in high school.

A blushing Audrey had shared those five words and no more.

We also met in high school. I thought to myself
he couldn't like me, but apparently he did.

I stopped typing and told Lily, "That one was from my cousin
Lexi. Audrey was happy that Lexi was so eager to tell her story
because *she* didn't want to say anything else about Jake."

We dated in college, broke up, and got back
together about ten years later.

We met at our fifteen-year high school reunion.

I then added my mom and dad's story and my grandparents'
stories. We were finished with Group One.

Group Two - Situations that could happen now:

We've known each other since we were three.

Lily and I thought of all of the boys we knew when we were
three. I couldn't see it, and neither could she.

We were next-door neighbors.

We were friends at camp and started dating.

We met at band practice.

As you can see from above, our couples met in
many different ways, but there are three things
that we found in common with all of the stories:

1. All of the couples surveyed loved talking about themselves. In fact, we couldn't get some of them to stop talking about themselves.

2. They loved talking about how they met, how they almost didn't meet, and how they almost didn't go out with each other.

3. Most of those listening were always smiling while the couples told their "how we met" stories. People love hearing crush stories. They all look dreamy-eyed, like they are listening to fairy tales.

Now we went back to the millions of entries on the Internet for advice on how to get someone interested in dating you.

We hated all of the advice we found. After thinking about what to write, we added the following:

So how do you get someone to like you? How do you tell someone you like them?

We don't know. We do know that you have to do what is comfortable for you. All of our couples say that "it just happened," so we assume that it will just happen. Our gathered advice is this:

If you like someone, try to spend time with them, see if they want to spend time with you and when the time feels right tell them that you like them. Or if the time isn't right for you, maybe it will be right for your crush first.

The Internet did have a lot of good advice on what *not* to do.

Don't stalk your crush. Following them everywhere will just creep them out.

Realize that you can't make someone like you, in the same way that someone can't make you like them. They either do or they don't. Really.

Don't pretend to be someone that you aren't. You want someone to like you for you.

Don't continually text your crush. Wait for them to text you back. Texting them a lot will not make your crush like you more. If they don't respond, it is a good sign that they aren't interested.

Don't tell a lot of people that you like this person. It will just be embarrassing for you if they don't like you back.

If your crush doesn't like you, just move on. If you move on, you might open yourself up to finding that there is someone else out there who is trying to get to know you.

Don't forget to be real.

I was wiped out and relieved not to have to deal with the "liking" question anymore. Writing about "don't" advice is a lot easier than writing about "do" advice.

Lily took over.

> What do you do if someone likes you but you don't like them?

> When we went back to the Internet, we found a lot of mean advice that we ignored. This includes things that you should **never** do. For example **do not**

> Walk away from them whenever they are near you.

> Tell everyone you know that you don't like this person. Many of them will tell him or her.

> Send a mean text, e-mail or IM.

It was harder to find some kind advice. We finally found something good on wikiHow.

> So, what *do* you do if someone likes you and you don't like them in the same way?

> Tell the person privately that you only want to be friends. You don't have to be alone with them. You can send them a text or an e-mail, or tell them when they call you.

Never lead the other person on. Don't let them think that you like them in a boyfriend or girlfriend way, if you don't feel that way.

If they tell you that they like you, be nice. Make sure this person knows that you don't feel the same way, but in a kind way. You can say that it was very nice of them to tell you, but you don't feel the same way and you don't want to waste their energy on you.

This may sound really strange, but make sure that you really don't like the person before you tell them you're not interested. Maybe it surprised you that this person likes you and you may need a little time to figure out how you feel.

Also very important: you may like this person, but you just may not be ready to have a boyfriend or girlfriend. So don't do anything that you aren't ready to do.

Lily said to me, "I think that's how I feel about Jon right now. I'm just not ready."

We ended with the following points based on comments that we heard from everyone at Thanksgiving (not including, *Oh, I am soooo stuffed!*).

In general the important thing to remember with the "crushes' war" is to always be yourself and to never, ever let anyone treat you badly. If someone treats you badly, they don't deserve to be around you.

Lily stopped typing and smiled. "Guesssssss wha-at?" she said, drawing it out. "We are done with chapter nine, and I know what to do for ten."

I hugged her. "I don't even care what it is. Let's just do it. Tomorrow, please?"

11/28 - magnificent Monday

We were back at my kitchen table, hoping to finally finish. Lily said, "So here's what I think we should do. We have a bunch of leftover problems, and we have a leftover chapter. Let's throw these problems together into the last chapter so the readers will get some quick answers to some easyish-to-solve problems."

"I don't care at this point if we throw the rest of these problems in the blender and pour them on the paper. I'm so ready to be done with this!"

"Okay, then let's go for it! We'll set this chapter up as problems and strategies."

Lily typed:

CHAPTER TEN: Miscellaneous Missed Problems and Strategies

This is the chapter of leftovers. Like Thanksgiving, sometimes the leftovers are the best.

I liked it. "Perfect."

She looked at me, nodded, and continued:

> We have covered many topics, hopefully in depth, but there are some concerns that can be answered reasonably quickly, and we will include them here. Some of these suggestions might sound a little preachy, but since you are the reader, you can pick and choose what works for you.

"Let's preach away!" I said, happy that we were getting on with it.

We were back at the PBS website. "A lot of kids complain to PBS!" I said.

"Well, maybe they remember all the problems from *Sesame Street* and feel they have company," Lily joked. "Okay. Problemo numero uno."

"You're the boss on this one," I said.

> Problem 1: My mom or dad won't buy me cool clothes.
>
> Strategies
>
> a. Try to earn some money to buy the outfit you are interested in.
>
> b. Offer to do a chore in the house that your parent really hates as a trade for the cool jeans. (Warning: the chore could be really gross.)

Lily then started to recount some of the really gross chores in her house. We decided not to use any of those examples.

> c. Reason with her or him about why this purchase is so important.
>
> d. All of the above.
>
> Problem 2: My parents won't let me watch this show on TV that all of my friends are watching.

"It's so annoying when they do that," I said.
"Yeah, I know," Lily replied while she was typing.

> Strategies
>
> a. Try to explain to them that they were young once too. They may tell you that they never watched TV back then. They may tell you that they were never young. They will be exaggerating.
>
> b. You may be out of luck.
>
> Problem 3: When my parents have a fight, they don't speak to each other and send me back and forth with messages to each other.

I felt really bad when I reread this anonymous complaint, and I could tell that Lily did too.

Strategies

a. Tell your parents that you are not a hockey puck and they need to talk to each other, because it makes you feel bad when you have to be a go-between.

b. Ask another relative if they can help you out and speak to your parents about not putting you in the middle.

c. This could be a really serious issue that you feel is too hard to handle. Speaking with your guidance counselor about the problem may be the thing to do.

"My fingers are about to explode!" said Lily. "Could you take over?"

"Yup. We're not leaving this kitchen until this chapter is done!" I scooted over to the keyboard.

Problem 4: My parents say my texting is out of control. They could be right. What do I do?

Strategies

a. Try not to take your phone with you every-where you go.

"Yeah, good luck with that," Lily said while I continued typing.

b. Try not to let texting take the place of hanging out with your friends. If you are texting a lot with one of your friends, make a plan to get together instead.

c. Other kids might think that it is rude to text back and forth with one friend if you are hanging out with another. Try to be sensitive to how they feel.

d. Make sure you never text rude, mean, or gossipy things to anyone.

e. Don't text at dinner and limit texting when you are in a group setting. You will be more polite and be texting less.

Lily looked at our leftover list. "Ah! The fun one. Frenemies," she said. She got up and twirled across the kitchen singing "frenemies, frenemies," to the tune of *Jingle Bells*.

"Get back here," I said, "and tell me what to type."

"Okay!" She pulled out some notes and showed me some sites, and I typed:

Problem 5: How do I know if one or more of my friends is really a "frenemy"?

Here are some signs:

a. They don't enjoy hearing about something good that happens to you. They are not happy for your happiness.

b. They give you backhanded compliments. These are compliments that hurt your feelings. Examples include:

That's a cool shirt. I'm glad you finally got something new.

If I were you, I'd be happy that they are paying attention to you.

c. They gossip about you.

d. They try to ruin your friendships with other people.

e. They say they're helping you, but they really are not.

"Audrey told me that she had two so-called friends come over after school one day when she was in eighth grade. They went through her closet and told her what she could wear and what she couldn't wear. She told my mom, and Mom said those friends *wore* out their welcome. Audrey, of course, told Mom how lame that was, but she got the message. She didn't spend much time with those girls afterward."

"They told her what to wear, and they wore out their welcome. I like it," Lily said.

"Figures," I said. "And now for how to deal with frenemies."

Problem 6: What do I do if I have a frenemy?

Strategies

a. Talk to them about how you feel. Tell them they are hurting your feelings and give them a chance to change.

b. Realize that you may not be able to keep this friendship. If they are so negative, you may not want them around.

c. Make sure that you haven't been behaving the same way. 'Frenemyness' can rub off.

"Another new word!" said Lily. I looked up from typing and smiled.

Then I thought that everyone should be lucky enough to find their own Lily. Maybe that's also what it means to be your own best friend: Letting people who are really good to you come into your life.

Lily said, "*Weeell?* What are you so happy about?"

I became a little shy. "I'm ready for a break. Could you take over?"

"You know. I'm kind of tired," Lily said. "Let's save this for next time."

"Yeah, okay." I wanted to get this over and done with, but I was ready to stop as well. "We'll finish next time."

12/5 - not-so-magnificent Monday

With Thanksgiving over and winter break starting to peep over the horizon, we were too distracted to think about the last part of our final chapter. Somehow our distraction turned into a week. We were now really feeling pressure to get the project done. Ms. Lamb (bah!) wanted us to include a section on Internet safety and we were feeling very uninspired.

I had been thinking that it would be great to do a Secret Santa. We had a group big enough to make it really work. We could pick names from a bag and then get a gift and leave wrapped clues in different places so our person could figure out who their gift was coming from.

At lunch today with Imani, Sara, Amy, and Lily, I brought up the idea. "So guys, what do you think about doing a Secret Santa this year?" I asked.

"Fun! I'm in." Imani said.

There were a bunch of *me too*'s and we all started to plan when to pick names, how much to spend, how many clues to leave, and so on. We were all so busy talking that we didn't notice that Lily was really quiet.

"I think I'll pass," Lily said.

"Oh, c'mon," I said.

"Nope. Don't want to."

"Oh, it's gonna be really fun."

"I said no thanks."

"Why would you want to bail on this?" I asked. I was too excited about the plan to notice that Lily was getting tense.

"You know," Lily said, really annoyed, "you just don't take no for an answer." She got up and left the table. Everyone looked uncomfortable and ate their lunch quietly.

I was surprised and angry, and also kind of embarrassed. Lily had called me out over something that shouldn't have been a big deal. "Well, okay, guys, we'll just do it without her!" We decided that we would pull names later in the week. Things felt very strange, but we just chatted about other stuff.

I walked into language arts, sat down, and looked over at Lily, who just ignored me. All of our "fair fights with friends" advice just flew out the window. *It's really easy to tell others what to do. It's another thing to follow all of that advice,* I thought.

We were supposed to be working on our project, and Ms. Lamb noticed that we weren't doing anything. When she walked over to us and asked why we hadn't started, I opened the laptop and just began working. "I'm going to do the last topic in ten on Internet safety," I said. "We don't have to talk. I don't have anything to say to you right now anyway."

I started to look at our notes and filled in safety tips. Lily looked off in the other direction. I added the info and decided that she could look it over or not. I didn't care. Class ended, and we went our separate ways. When school was over, I hung out with Sara. She tried to talk to me about Lily, but I didn't want to hear anything about her. I left school and started to walk home. The wind was really howling.

I was near Lily's block when I heard her call me.

"Hey, Gaby." I ignored her and kept walking.

"Hey—wait up!" she said.

I turned around and said meanly, "Hey what?"

"I want to talk to you."

"Now you want to talk—where you can't embarrass me like you did at lunch."

"Just give me a chance."

"Okay, what?"

"You know, it's really cold out. Just come over."

I thought about whether I really felt like talking to Lily at that moment. I looked at her and also decided she didn't look like the confident Lily I saw most of the time. She looked more like an anxious Lily that I really didn't see very often.

"Well, okay, but you better tell me what's up."

We went to Lily's. No one was home, so we texted our moms to let them know we were at her house.

"What on earth is your problem?" I demanded.

Lily almost looked like she was going to cry. She bit her lip. I was surprised but still kind of annoyed with her.

"So," Lily said, after she calmed down. "Last year, when you were so busy with those friends of yours, I was sort of friendly with some kids I knew for a long time."

I remembered some of the kids. I was never friendly with them. They were a very tight group that came from another elementary school. "Yeah, what about it?"

Lily paused. "Do you want me to tell you or not?"

"Yeah, tell me."

"Anyway, I was friendly with them. They were okay some of the time. They left me out a lot, but they were the ones that I knew and I wasn't comfortable looking for some new friends." She took a deep breath. "We planned to do a Secret Santa, and there were two kids that wanted to do it with us, but the rest of the girls didn't want them to join in. I thought that I would speak up for them. Well, the group finally said, 'Sure, they can join, but why don't you go find some other kids to boss around.' They all left me out. Even the ones that I thought I was helping wouldn't speak up for me. I started being left out more and more and was pretty much on my own by the end of last year. Things have been going pretty well for me this year, so why should I start up with this Santa stuff all over again?"

I remembered seeing Lily alone a lot last year. She was one of those kids I automatically stayed away from—the unpopular kind. I looked at her and before I even thought any further, I said, "You know, Lily, I wouldn't ever leave you out, and neither would AIS."

Lily said, "I want to show you something." We went upstairs to her room. She disappeared into her closet and started rummaging around. She pulled out a bag with a bunch of little wrapped items. "This was my secret Santa bag from last year. I was really excited to get the gift and clues wrapped so I bought everything ahead of time. When I was left out, I hid the bag in the closet where my mom wouldn't see it."

I looked at all of the wrapped stuff and felt bad for how she had been treated last year. "Well, it would be a real shame to let all of those clues and wrapping go to waste…so why don't you use it this year!"

"I have no clue what's in there!" Lily said, looking a little less upset.

"Then it should be a real surprise. It can be a double Secret Santa!" We both laughed.

"Okay, Gaby. I'll do it."

We sat quietly for a bit. Then she said, "Sorry about being mean at lunch."

"We'll call this your one freebie," I said. "Hey, let's look at what I did for the Internet safety section and finish this chapter."

Lily and I looked it over and added some information from the Safekids.com website:

Problem 7: How can I be "safe" on the Internet?

Strategies

a. Don't ever give out personal information, like addresses or phone numbers, without checking with your parents first.

b. If you come across something that makes you feel uncomfortable, tell your parents right away.

c. Check with your parents before posting any pictures of yourself.

d. Don't respond to any mean messages.

e. Don't give out your passwords to anyone but your parents.

f. Don't download anything without checking with your parents first.

g. You may have to teach your parents or grandparents how to use the Internet. They'll owe you!

Then we knew it. We were done!

12/6—not-time-yet Tuesday

As soon as language arts started today, we went straight to Ms. Lamb and told her that we thought our book was finished.

She said, "Great." Then she said to the class, "Everyone, don't forget to include an introduction with your books. It doesn't have to be any more than a few lines." She added happily, "Grammar workshop today! Please take out your binders."

How she could sound excited about this was beyond me.

I whispered to Lily, "Do these teachers just plan for more torture or what? Hey, just come over today and let's get the introduction done so we can hand it in, okay?"

"Yeah, I'll check with my mom after school," Lily said.

We walked home. You could tell that winter was coming. The sky had that bright, gray look, and it smelled like snow. I mentioned this to Lily.

"How do you smell snow?" she asked.

"It's an art," I said. "We'll save that question for the next book!" Lily rolled her eyes.

After a quick snack at my house, Lily said, "Go!" I googled famous quotes and came up with a plan.

Introduction

To quote famous people (sort of):

Middle school can be the best of times and the worst of times.

Happy middle school students are all alike. Every unhappy middle school student is unhappy in his or her own way.

Justice? You get justice in the next world. In this world you have middle school.

Thanks and apologies to authors Charles Dickens, Leo Tolstoy, and William Gaddis for letting us use and destroy their quotes, but they really all show something that we have learned in writing this book.

When we wrote this book, we spoke to everyone we knew. We spoke to our parents, their friends, our relatives, our friends, and our friends' sisters and brothers and their friends, and we learned that every problem in this book is a universal problem. They don't happen only in middle school. They happen throughout life. Some problems we grow out of, only to grow back into them.

Regardless of what the problem is, you sometimes just have to be prepared to be your own best friend, stay strong for yourself, and always remember that these problems won't be with you forever. If you have a problem, catch your breath and know that if today isn't so good, tomorrow or the day after will be better.

I looked up. Lily said, "Works for me, Gaby. But you know that for all of the other times that aren't 'sometimes,' you're my best friend."

"Works for me," I said.

Lily saved the file and sent *The Best Middle School Self-Defense Book Ever* to Ms. Lamb. I printed the hard copy that we also needed to hand in. Lily was still busy at the keyboard, so I asked her, "What are you doing?"

"I'm sending a copy to your sister."

"You're *what?*" I asked.

"Remember, she wanted to see it."

I didn't want to ruin our warm moment of friendship and the great feeling of being finished, so I didn't give Lily a hard time, but I really wasn't sure that I wanted Audrey to read the book. Oh well. Too late.

Lily went home. I finished my homework and had an uneventful dinner with my family, so happy to be done with the project.

After dinner, I was hanging out in my room, and Audrey popped her head in. "Guess what I have?" she asked in that tone that could only mean trouble.

"I know," I said. "You have the book. Don't be too mean."

"I'm going to read it right now," she said, and bounced out of the bedroom.

I sat with Scout and stared at the ceiling. After about fifteen minutes, I walked by her room. She was sitting on her bed, hunched over her laptop, with the glow of the screen lighting up her face...and she was smiling! I pretended to look for something in the bathroom and walked by again. I overheard, "Hmm," and "Hah!" and more "Hmm."

After about another half hour, I didn't think I could take it anymore, but just then she walked by my room and said, "Clique virus! I just love it!"

12/21—winding-up Wednesday

The past weeks have been busy ones. Finals, holiday school performances, lots of talk about vacation plans, a Secret Santa success, and...buzz!

Audrey apparently wasn't the only one who read the book. She e-mailed it to a bunch of her friends (leaving our names off of it). She wrote, "Check out this middle school survival guide." Her friends read it and forwarded it to some others, and on and on. Over the next few weeks, we started to see and hear some very familiar things take place.

One day Lily told me that she heard a teacher coming out of the lounge saying to another teacher, "Well, that clique has mutated!"

Another day we saw some kids playing a new game. One would name a teenage movie character, and then others would race to the Internet, trying to figure out how old the actor really was when he or she played that role.

Last week Audrey told me that she overheard a kid in her grade talking about someone and saying, "Oh yeah, she's a number four in that clique."

Kids in the eighth grade were lobbying for Power Nap Day once a week (and they meant all day).

At lunch today Imani told us that she overheard a girl tell her friends, "Do I have a great crush war story for you!"

I thought that the book was starting some new trends. I didn't mention this to Lily because it sounded dorky, but I felt very cool about the whole thing.

"We've gone viral," Lily said. I had to agree. Both the middle school and high school were buzzing about things in the book.

We walked to Ms. Lamb's class and sat down, waiting for her to hand back our graded projects. She walked around the room and dropped different partners' projects at their desks. When she stopped by us, she smiled. "Great job, you two." She handed us our book and then moved on to the next group. We had gotten an A.

"And now it's time to discuss the spring project." The whole class started moaning. "You'll be working in teams of four. You can keep your partner and add two more people, or you can start a new group."

We didn't have to hear anymore. We just exchanged a look and knew that we would work together. We didn't know the topic yet, but it didn't matter. I didn't care who else might work with us, but already Jon and Ted had motioned to us, so I guessed that we were set.

"Decide on your groups by the start of spring semester. When you get back to school after vacation, we'll discuss book ideas." Ms. Lamb continued, ignoring the groans coming from various corners of the classroom.

"All I can say is thank goodness for winter break," said Lily as we walked home from school. I had to agree. But I also thought back on the past few months. I had started the year feeling so alone and hurt. It took some time for things to change, but I really lucked out with the chance to work on *The Best Middle School Self-Defense Book Ever* and hang out with Lily. She had always been around, but I never thought of her as someone to have as a friend. Now, it was hard to imagine not knowing her.

"Yeah," I said. "I'm so ready for there to be no school for a while. Hey, do you want to plan a New Year's Eve sleepover party?"

"Sure," Lily said. "Also, I was thinking about a bunch of us going ice skating one day over break." We walked on, quiet for a bit.

Winter break is going to be great. I plan to have a blast and not miss school at all. I know that when I get back to school in January, Lily won't be hiding from me the way Taylor and Lins did in September. I also know that I'll be able to deal with problems that come up.

Middle school life will be much more tolerable. It might even be fun.

Gaby and Lily's Chapters for
The Best Middle School Self-Defense
Book Ever

Acknowledgements

Thanks to Larry, Jess, and Ali for their encouragement, editing, and for providing so much fodder for this story. Thanks to Mattie and Lisa for their support of the book. Thanks to Craig for setting an example for me.

Thank you, Amy Laburda, for fitting this project in with all of your other work commitments.

Also, heartfelt gratitude to Helen DiNetta for her patience, editing, and friendship. Thanks for getting me here, in so many ways.

Linda Elkin, New York, 2014